**Exquisite ecstasy
surged through her**

"Kyle, please don't!" Tricia cried in a
choked voice as she wrenched her
mouth from his.

"I've proved something, haven't I?" he
stated thickly, beads of perspiration
standing out on his forehead.

"You've proved nothing except that
there's an undeniable physical
attraction between us," Tricia
said defiantly.

"Will it satisfy you to have only the
surface of your emotions skimmed
when you know you can reach the
heights with me?" Kyle demanded.
The note of intimacy in his voice
quickened her pulse and sent the
blood flowing more swiftly through
her veins.

"No, it won't always satisfy me!" Tricia
wanted to cry out, but instead she
looked away. Kyle spoke of desire. Not
once during their entire relationship
had he ever mentioned the
word *love*.

YVONNE WHITTAL
is also the author of these

Harlequin Presents

and these

Harlequin Romances

Many of these books are available at your local bookseller.

For a free catalog listing all titles currently available,
send your name and address to:

HARLEQUIN READER SERVICE
1440 South Priest Drive, Tempe, AZ 85281
Canadian address: Stratford, Ontario N5A 6W2

YVONNE WHITTAL

the silver falcon

Harlequin Books

TORONTO • NEW YORK • LOS ANGELES • LONDON
AMSTERDAM • PARIS • SYDNEY • HAMBURG
STOCKHOLM • ATHENS • TOKYO • MILAN

Harlequin Presents first edition May 1983
ISBN 0-373-10598-3

Original hardcover edition published in 1983
by Mills & Boon Limited

CHAPTER ONE

THE early morning sunlight slanted in through the office window and fell across the worn persian carpet. Dusty files, no longer in use and kept mainly for sentimental reasons, lined the shelves against the one wall, and reminders and out-of-date schedules were pinned untidily to the notice board behind the large old stinkwood desk. Photographs of Knysna during the 1830s hung against the remaining walls, adding to the old-worldly atmosphere of the room, while the smell of newly sawn timber seemed to cloy the air.

None of this was new to Tricia Meredith as she sat with her head lowered over the notepad resting on her knee, while her pencil flew across the paper as she took down the letters Charles Barrett was dictating. The whining of the power saws, the rumbling and revving of the lumber trucks, and the droning of the cranes stacking the lengths of timber in the stockyard to await transport had become part of her daily existence during the past six years. In the factory beyond the mill handmade stinkwood furniture was being produced to lure the tourist trade, and Tricia had spent many a lunch hour admiring the craftsmanship of the workers. She would perhaps have earned more had she gone somewhere else, but she enjoyed working for Charles Barrett, and he and his wife, Milly, had been good to her over the years.

'I think that's enough for this morning,' her employer's deep, gravelly voice announced after a pause, and Tricia looked up to see him frowning down at the blotter on his desk.

She knew him well enough to have guessed that something had been troubling him over the past weeks, and although she was concerned and curious, she stopped short of prying.

'I'll type these letters at once, Mr Barrett.'

'Later.' The unusual abruptness of his voice startled her momentarily, and she paused on her way to the door to see him gesture vaguely towards the chair she had just vacated. 'Sit down, Tricia. There's something I must tell you before you hear it from someone else.'

Tricia resumed her seat quietly, but an inexplicable wariness was taking possession of her. 'What is it, Mr Barrett?'

For a moment he said nothing, almost as if he were searching for the right words, but then he sighed and said bluntly, 'I've sold the business.'

Tricia had expected it to be something serious, but never *this*, and, too stunned to speak, she sat staring at him a little stupidly while she assimilated the shocking news.

'But why?' she asked eventually. 'Barrett's has been in your family for so many years, and——' She broke off abruptly and shook her head so that the soft, dark curls bounced slightly about her slim shoulders. 'I don't understand.'

'I don't have a son to carry on after me, Tricia,' he explained tiredly, 'and you know as well as I do that the profit margin has decreased steadily over the past year. With the economic situation as it is, small companies such as mine don't stand a chance against the larger timber companies. Besides ...' Charles Barrett passed a shaky hand over his grey, thinning hair and smiled a little wanly, 'it's time I retired to that little cottage my wife and I have had in mind for some months now.'

Tricia lowered her glance to the notepad she clutched in her hands and unobtrusively blinked away the film of tears in her eyes. 'Barrett's won't be the same without you.'

'It's kind of you to say so, Tricia,' her employer replied in a voice that sounded distinctly wavery with emotion. 'If I could have chosen, then I would have stayed on until I dropped like my father before me, but I received an excellent offer for the business which I couldn't refuse, and this way I'm at least assured of a certain amount of comfort in my old age.'

'You're not old, Mr Barrett,' Tricia argued, her warm, golden-brown eyes surveying him critically across the wide expanse of the desk.

Charles Barrett smiled faintly and neatly clipped off the end of his cigar before lighting it. 'I'll be sixty-five this coming summer, Tricia, and I'm too old to fight against the odds. This way Barrett's can go on into prosperity with the power of Union Timber behind it.'

'*Union Timber?*' Tricia felt as if everything within her had ceased to function except for the soaring, throbbing sensation in her head, and, with a stricken look on her ashen face, she stammered, 'But that's—that's——'

'Kyle Hammond's company, yes,' Charles Barrett filled in for her when her voice came to a jerky stop. 'He'll be coming down to Knysna next week to sort out the final details for the take-over.'

Kyle Hammond. He was the dynamic force behind Union Timber, a company that had, over the past years, been swallowing up smaller companies in South Africa from Cape Agulhas up to the Limpopo, and now Barrett's had been placed on the menu. Kyle Hammond also happened to be the one person who despised Tricia enough to want to destroy her if he could, and now he was, indirectly, going to be her employer. She had hoped their paths would never cross again, but fate obviously had other plans, and the comfortable little world she had created for herself was suddenly being threatened with extinction.

'It's been six years, Tricia,' Charles Barrett remarked, guessing her thoughts with his remarkable shrewdness. 'No one, not even Kyle Hammond, could bear a grudge over such a lengthy period.'

'Kyle Hammond has a memory like a computer,' she replied bitterly. 'He never forgets, and he never forgives.'

'He won't thank you for remaining silent.'

'He won't thank me for revealing the truth either,' Tricia sighed, rising from her chair on shaky legs. 'I'll get these letters typed.'

In the small adjoining office she inserted a sheet of paper into the typewriter, but she sat for a long time staring blankly at her shorthand notes while her fingers rested idly on the keys. The temptation to run was incredibly strong, but nothing would give Kyle Hammond more pleasure than to know that she feared him.

Her fingers made an involuntary movement towards the silver falcon that hung on a chain about her neck, and her own youthful, happy voice echoed back from the past to haunt her.

'It's the first real gift I've ever received, and I shall wear it always, Kyle, because it reminds me of you.'

She dragged her thoughts back to the present with a shuddering sigh. She did not want to think of Kyle and of those brief, exquisite moments they had once shared before her fragile bubble of happiness had been shattered so cruelly. She did not want to think of the past, but the past and the present had suddenly become fused into one to uncover painful memories she would have given anything to forget.

Tricia never quite knew how she managed to get through the rest of that day until it was time for her to drive herself home to her small flat overlooking the lagoon, and even then, surrounded by the odd bits of furniture she had lovingly collected over the years, she found no relief from her thoughts. She took a leisurely bath and changed into something more comfortable before making herself something to eat, but she was so tense that she almost screamed when her doorbell rang shrilly shortly after eight that evening.

Frank Carlson stood on her doorstep and his craggy face lit up in a dear, familiar smile as she let him in. Frank owned the garage a few blocks away from her flat, and over the years he had drifted into her life in that quiet, unassuming way of his. She had grown fond of this solid, dependable man with his simple, uncomplicated manner, and she knew that, in his way, he cared for her very deeply. Proposing to her, and being refused, had almost become a ritual, but Frank had remained her undaunted companion through it all.

'I'm glad you came,' she said in that faintly husky voice of hers as she led the way into her small lounge.

'I had a feeling you might need me,' he announced calmly, and she swung round to face him, her eyes wide and dark in her pale face.

'You've always had the uncanny knack of knowing my every mood,' she said jerkily, and then, as the tension snapped inside her, she burst into tears.

Quite unperturbed, Frank took her into his arms and offered the comfort of his broad shoulder for her to cry on. He spoke to her soothingly after a time, and made her sit down on the small sofa, but he kept his arm about her while she made use of his handkerchief when her tears ceased.

'I'm sorry, Frank,' she sniffed into the white linen, raising her head from his shoulder where the familiar smell of pipe tobacco and after-shave lotion clung to him. 'I don't know what's the matter with me. I don't usually behave this way.'

'Could it have something to do with Kyle Hammond and Barrett's?' that deep, calm voice of his questioned her unexpectedly, and she looked up sharply to find his grey eyes surveying her intently.

'Has someone been keeping you informed?'

'No, but I saw Kyle Hammond and Charles Barrett coming out of the Queen's Hotel a few evenings ago. They were both carrying briefcases, and they looked very businesslike. I put two and two together, and ...' He paused briefly, his eyes flicking over her tear-stained face. 'Is Union Timber taking over Barrett's?'

'Yes,' she admitted without hesitation, 'but keep it to yourself for the time being. Kyle will be here some time next week to finalise the transaction, and then I suppose the whole of Knysna will know.'

Frank stared at her thoughtfully for a time before he was forced to rescue his handkerchief from being mangled between her agitated fingers. 'Is it the thought of seeing Kyle again that has upset you so?'

'He hates me, Frank, for what he thinks I did to his father.'

'And you, Tricia? How do you feel about him now?'

'I ... don't know,' she frowned, her small, slender hands fluttering vaguely before she clasped them tightly in her lap. 'Six years is a long time. People change, and I was only nineteen at the time.'

She sat staring at the carpet for some time, trying to analyse her feelings, but coming up against a blank wall of fear each time. She feared his cold hatred, and what he might do to her when he discovered that she was still an employee of Barrett's, but most of all she feared the power he possessed to hurt her more deeply than anyone else in the world.

'You can't run away from the past, Tricia. It has a nasty habit of catching up with you when you least expect it, and there's really only one thing you can do about it,' Frank advised calmly. 'Face it, and fight it.'

'I have no weapons with which to fight.'

'You have the truth on your side.'

'I could never tell him the truth,' she cried passionately. 'Never!'

'He'll have to know eventually,' Frank insisted.

'Well, he won't hear it from me!'

Frank took out his pipe and lit it carefully in his usual unhurried manner before his shrewd glance met Tricia's. 'You still love him, don't you?'

His calm statement shook her considerably. Could she still love a man she had not seen for six years? Could there still be one iota of feeling left for a man who had despised her from the moment they had met, and who had eventually hurt her more than she cared to remember? Her mind gave her an instant reply, but her heart was hesitant.

Her breath came out in a long, quivering sigh and, getting to her feet, she placed her arms about herself in a vaguely protective gesture as she paced the floor. 'What am I going to do?'

'You could always marry me,' he suggested with an underlying seriousness to the humorous twinkle in his grey eyes, and she smiled for the first time that day since hearing of the take-over.

'You're a dear, Frank.' She leaned over him and kissed him lightly on his leathery cheek. 'But it wouldn't work, and you know it.'

'Tricia——'

'I feel much better now that I've shared the news with you,' she interrupted hastily, drawing away from him and changing the subject. 'Could I make you a cup of coffee?'

His lips tightened for a moment, but then his familiar smile broke through. 'You know I never refuse a cup of coffee, and you also know that you can't always refuse *me*, Tricia.'

Frank's statement disturbed her slightly, but he did not stay long after he had had his coffee. When he left, however, he pulled her close and kissed her with more warmth than usual.

'I'll always be there if you should need me,' he said gruffly, and a few moments later the lift doors closed behind him.

Tricia sighed guiltily as she locked the door to her flat and turned out the lights. There had been times when she had leaned heavily on Frank for support, and he had given it unstintingly, but she felt ashamed when she thought of how little she had given in return. She had tried very hard to love him, but she had been forced to admit that that vital spark was missing in their relationship. She loved him like one loved an older brother. But as a husband, and lover? No!

That night, for the first time in years, she could not prevent herself from thinking back on the past in its entirety, and, as she lay on her bed staring into the darkness, she saw it all vividly, so vividly that every memory brought with it its own unique pain.

She had known very little about her grandmother who had looked after her for a few years after her parents had died, but she remembered clearly being taken to the orphanage when she was barely six years old. She could still recall the unfamiliar smell of the place, the dark, frighteningly long passages, the creaking springs of the narrow bed with its hard, lumpy mattress, and the shutters at the tall windows that banged incessantly on a windy night. There were other children there, of course, who were as homeless as herself, but that did not diminish her sensitivity, her loneliness, and her longing for the warmth and security of her own home and family.

During her last year at school the orphanage children had been treated to a week's holiday at Knysna with its forests, and its lagoon, and its magnificent view of the sea beyond the two sandstone cliffs at the Knysna Heads. This was where she wanted to live, she had decided at once, and after completing her year at the secretarial college she had packed all her possessions into one small suitcase and had taken the train to Knysna.

Within less than a week she had found herself employed in the offices at Barrett's Timber Mill, and her cheap little room in one of the town's respectable boarding houses had felt like an extravagantly furnished suite in a five-star hotel.

Tricia spent every available moment exploring the sights in and around Knysna, and it was on that fateful summer's day, towards the end of January, that she encountered Benjamin Hammond leaning heavily against the bonnet of his Mercedes in the Coney Glen Nature Reserve. His face was a bluish-white as he struggled to breathe, and Tricia had gone to his aid at once.

'Tablets!' he gasped, gesturing towards the glove compartment of the car when she had loosened his tie, and helped him into the front seat.

She found the small phial of tablets without difficulty and helped him to take one with the little water she still had left in the flask in her rucksack.

'That's better,' he said at length when his colour returned to normal, and a wavery smile curved his now relaxed mouth. 'I shouldn't have come out here on my own, I know, but I'm deeply grateful to you, young lady. You saved my life.'

'I'm glad,' Tricia said simply, brushing the dark, feathery curls out of her eyes as she sat down cross-legged on the wild grass beside the car and stared up at the elderly man who sat straightening his tie and pushing shaky fingers through his white hair. 'I'm Patricia Meredith,' she introduced herself, her usual shyness forgotten.

'I'm Benjamin Hammond,' he reciprocated with a warm smile. 'And I'm very glad to know you, Miss Meredith.'

'My friends call me Tricia.'

'Tricia,' he sampled her name slowly, and then he smiled again, his hazel eyes taking in her sturdy boots, the dusty denims covering shapely legs, and the red checkered cotton blouse. 'How did you get up here to Coney Glen?'

'I hiked.'

His heavy eyebrows rose sharply. 'It's a very long way from Knysna.'

'I know,' Tricia laughed, shaking the dust out of her khaki bush hat and placing it unceremoniously on her head so that the soft, sagging brim shaded her eyes from the bright sunlight. 'I've always enjoyed hiking.'

'How old are you?' he asked. 'Or is that a question I shouldn't ask a young lady such as yourself?'

'I don't mind,' she smiled shyly. 'I'm nineteen.'

'And your parents? Do they live here in Knysna?'

'My parents are dead,' she said with a casualness she had adopted over the years. She tasted the tangy freshness of the sea on her lips and stared out across the flower-bedecked veld towards the Indian Ocean. 'My father died before I was born, and my mother died giving birth to me.'

'You grew up in an orphanage?'

'Yes.'

Tricia had always been withdrawn and uncommunicative, but for some strange reason she found it easy to talk to Benjamin Hammond. He questioned her about herself, and told her more about himself than she imagined he had intended to, and then he had shared her meagre lunch with her. He eventually insisted on driving her back into town, and she took it for granted that she had seen the last of him, but a few days later she received an invitation to dine with him at his holiday home one evening. A car was sent to pick her up, and the holiday cottage she had expected turned out to be a mansion nestling among the trees, and surrounded by spacious grounds in which sparkling fountains took pride of place. The interior was just as impressive with its priceless *objets d'art* and antique furnishings, and Tricia was totally overwhelmed by Benjamin Hammond's obvious wealth. She had never seen or imagined such luxury before, and her pretty chiffon evening dress, bought especially for the occasion out of her savings, seemed suddenly cheap and out of place. The large double doors opened to admit her into the spacious living-room, and at that moment she would have fled in panic had Benjamin Hammond's warm, friendly voice not requested her to enter.

Ensconced in a deep, winged armchair with a non-alcoholic drink on the low, marble-topped table beside him, he held out both his thin hands in a welcoming gesture, and Tricia went forward at once to place her hands in his.

'I'm so glad you could come,' he said simply.

Tricia smiled down at him nervously and said with innate truthfulness, 'If I'd known that you lived in such splendour, I would have hesitated to accept your kind invitation.'

'Don't let this outward show of wealth frighten you, my child,' he grunted with touching sincerity. 'I'm the same old man who nearly collapsed at your feet up there on Coney Glen, and I'd like to repay you in some small way for your kindness that day, and your generosity in allowing me to share your lunch.'

His son and stepdaughter entered the living-room before Tricia could reply, and she discovered that Maxine, a year younger than herself, was titian-haired, pretty, thoroughly spoiled, and an inherent snob as Benjamin Hammond had warned. It was Kyle Hammond's autocratic appearance, however, that made Tricia feel as though she had been dealt a severe and fatal blow to the heart.

At the age of twenty-six Kyle had emanated a virility and a raw masculinity she had never encountered before in the almost cloistered life she had led before coming to Knysna, and, inexperienced as she was, she had felt the first stirrings of an emotion she could not yet understand.

Tall, lean and muscular in his dark, impeccably tailored suit, he looked a long way down his aristocratic nose at her to make her squirm uncomfortably beneath the penetrating stare of those peculiar tawny eyes. There was animosity there, and suspicion, but it was the colour of his hair that made her glance at him more than once that evening throughout dinner. Against the superb tan of his chiselled features his hair was so strikingly fair that it was almost silver in the light of the chandelier hanging above the dinner table.

Tricia had been so aware of him that she hardly

knew what she had eaten, but Kyle made it quite clear what he thought of her, and when they had a moment alone together he seized the opportunity to accuse her quite blatantly of striking up a friendship with his father in order to benefit financially. He had had to deal with gold-diggers before, and he would have no compunction in dealing with her in the harshest manner if she stepped out of line, he had said, and, shocked to the very core of her being, she had been unable to utter a word in her own defence.

She had left, that evening, feeling angry and hurt, and if she had had any sense she would have stayed away after that, but Benjamin Hammond suffered a mild coronary thrombosis the following day, and she found that she did not have the heart to ignore his repeated requests to see her. After that there was no turning back.

Kyle's animosity grew towards Tricia during the weeks that followed, and he made no secret of the fact that he disliked her presence in the house on the numerous occasions she called to see his father. He was suspicious of the many hours she spent talking to Benjamin, or playing his favourite game of chess with him, and he made use of every opportunity to insult her. Tricia should have hated Kyle for the many barbed, unkind remarks he directed at her, but instead she fell in love with him with all the youthful passion of her young heart. He was like a silver god to her—untouchable, proud and magnificent, and she observed him often with a hungry yearning she could not even begin to explain to herself.

The bond of friendship that was forged between

Benjamin Hammond and Tricia remained a thorn
in Kyle's side, and Maxine, although she never said
anything, disliked Tricia with equal intensity.
Neither Maxine nor Kyle would have understood
what Benjamin's friendship meant to a lonely, sensitive girl like Tricia, and neither would they have
understood what her companionship meant to a
man like Benjamin who had thought that he had
nothing more of himself to give to anyone.

With Maxine away at her modelling classes most
of the time, and Kyle in Cape Town taking care of
the company business, they gradually began to realise what Tricia's companionship meant to their
father. Kyle's aggressively suspicious manner dimin-
ished, and Tricia's adulation grew with the crumbs
of friendliness that fell her way. This made no difference to the fact that Kyle disliked her intensely, and
yet there were times when she caught him observing
her with a look in his eyes that sent the blood rushing freely through her veins.

Their eyes had met and held one Sunday evening
across the sleeping form of his father, and in the
throbbing silence that had followed it had felt to
Tricia as if their souls had reached out to intertwine
and become one. The experience had left her feeling curiously weak, and she did not protest when
Kyle offered to drive her home, but her heart was
thudding heavily when he stopped the car unexpectedly along the way to kiss her. It was the first
time a man's lips had ever touched hers, and when
he finally dropped her off at the entrance to the
boarding house, her heart was still beating so fast
that she could hardly breathe.

She could still feel the imprint of that firm, hard

mouth against her soft lips as she hurried inside, and that night her childish dreams were centred on Kyle; a very different Kyle from the harsh, censorious man she had first met.

When Tricia arrived at Benjamin Hammond's house shortly after lunch the following Saturday, she found Kyle waiting for her on the terrace, and her heart seemed to somersault in her breast at the sight of him.

'I have something for you,' he said, and when his hand emerged from his jacket pocket she found herself staring at a small silver charm dangling at the end of the silver chain which he held between his strong, lean fingers.

It was a falcon with its wings spread in flight, and its claws extended to scoop up its prey. It was somehow symbolical of Kyle, she thought. Silvery-haired and proud, he was very much a falcon, and she believed that he could be equally ruthless when in pursuit of something he desired.

She stood speechless while he fastened it about her throat, his fingers against her skin sending pleasurable little shivers along her spine that quickened her pulse, but, as he turned her about to face him, she fingered the charm lovingly and said: 'It's the first real gift I've ever received, and I shall wear it always, Kyle, because it reminds me of you.'

'Does it?' he replied cynically to her shy admittance. 'I rather thought it reminded me of you—a bird of prey circling its victim, and the victim is my father.'

Hurt and bewildered, she whispered hoarsely, 'You can't still think that I'm that sort of person.'

'Can't I?' His hands tightened on her shoulders

as he pulled her roughly towards him, but, as her softness made contact with his hard body, she saw an unfathomable expression flit across his face. 'What sort of person are you that you can make me doubt my own judgment?'

Before she could think of a suitable reply he had lowered his head, and for the second time in her life she found herself being kissed in that savagely demanding way that frightened and excited her simultaneously.

Kyle released her at the sound of approaching footsteps, and they turned to see Maxine walking towards them, her tight-fitting white slacks accentuating the faintly seductive sway of her hips. There was a smile on her lips, but the green eyes that met Tricia's were filled with undisguised hatred.

'Father is waiting for you,' she said, adopting the same tone of voice she used with the servants, but Tricia, slow to anger, chose to ignore it, and went inside without a backward glance at the two people who remained behind on the sunlit terrace.

Benjamin Hammond's thin face lit up with pleasure when she entered his room. 'Tricia, child, I'm so glad you came early. I was looking forward to a game of chess.'

She pulled up a chair and sat down opposite him. 'I'm in a fighting mood today, so prepare yourself for defeat.'

'So it's a battle you want, is it?'

'To the bitter end,' she smiled.

'Prepare for attack,' he replied humorously, advancing with his knight, and for the next two hours she was able to forget about Kyle and his disturbing behaviour.

Later that afternoon, when she left the house, she took the path down to the lagoon, knowing that Kyle had gone out in his yacht, and hoping that she might catch a glimpse of him coming in to the small jetty.

This desire just to see him was crazy, she told herself, but, as she came to the end of the wooded path and stepped out on to the sand, her heart almost stopped beating. The *Sea Sprite* was fastened to its moorings, and Kyle was on board, bending over what appeared to be the engine. She stood immobile, not sure what to do, and then he raised his head and looked directly at her as if he had felt her eyes on him. He lifted his hand in a mock salute, and, realising that it would be childish to pretend she had not seen him, she walked across the stretch of sand and on to the wooden jetty.

'Come aboard,' he said. 'You're just in time.'

'In time for what?' she asked nervously, unable to keep her eyes off the wide expanse of his gleaming, muscular shoulders and hair-roughened chest.

'I've had problems with the engine, and I'm taking her out for a trial run,' he explained, his arrogant, faintly mocking gaze holding hers as he walked towards her. 'You want to come along, don't you?'

'If you promise to have me back here within the hour,' she replied, not quite sure that she was doing the right thing.

His smile deepened, and a lazy finger traced the dusting of freckles across the bridge of her small, straight nose. 'Have you got a heavy date for this evening?'

She blushed for no reason at all and turned away

from his disturbing nearness. 'We have dinner at six in the boarding house.'

'We'll be back long before then,' he promised.

Tricia felt vaguely uneasy, but, as the high-powered engine of the *Sea Sprite* took them between the majestic Heads and out to sea, she began to relax and enjoy herself. It was a warm afternoon, and the tangy breeze whipped against her face until she tasted the salt of the sea on her lips. Seagulls screeched and swooped low overhead, and the swaying motion of the yacht lulled her into contentment. Kyle was at the helm, and, with his hair ruffled by the playful breeze, he looked almost boyish, she thought as she glanced at him covertly.

They must have been a couple of miles out to sea when the rhythmic throbbing of the *Sea Sprite*'s engine faltered. It spluttered to life again, missed a couple of strokes, and then it cut out completely so that only the sound of the sea could be heard.

Tricia's heart leapt into her throat and seemed to remain there while Kyle inspected the engine.

'I'm afraid you're going to be very late for dinner,' he said at last, straightening to frown down at her. '*Too* late, in fact.'

CHAPTER TWO

KYLE was still working on the engine when the sun dipped beyond the distant hills, and Tricia shivered as if someone had draped a cold wet blanket about her.

'You'd better get down below,' Kyle suggested, pulling on a knitted sweater. 'The nights are cold out at sea.'

'How long will it be before you have the engine repaired?' she asked, wrapping her arms about herself in an effort to keep warm, and feeling inordinately wary at the prospect of perhaps having to spend the night alone with him.

'Another hour at least,' he set her mind at ease as he adjusted the battery-operated lamp and glanced at her with a touch of wry humour on this face. 'I can think of pleasanter ways to spend a few hours out at sea with a pretty girl for company, but, considering the circumstances, perhaps you wouldn't mind rustling up something in the galley for us to eat while I get on with the repairs.'

Tricia felt her cheeks grow hot and turned away hastily to climb down the short flight of steps into the well-lit cabin. She closed the door behind her to keep out the cold, and looked about her a little helplessly, at first, before she searched the cupboards for the one containing the food supplies. There would be very little to prepare, she discovered, for it would merely be a case of opening up tins and warming the contents.

She sat for a moment, drinking in the silence which was disturbed only by the sound of the water lapping against the side of the yacht, but then, to overcome her nervous agitation, she laid the table and began the preparations for what would eventually prove to be an unforgettable dinner.

She could almost have cried with relief when the engine eventually throbbed into life. A knock on the cabin window made her spin about sharply to see Kyle giving her the thumbs-up sign, and a few moments later the engine was cut and he was entering the cabin. He washed his hands and combed his hair into place, but, as he passed her on his way to the table, he paused and placed a hand on her shoulder, his touch sending a flow of warmth through her.

'How are you going to explain this to your date?'

'I told you I haven't got a date, and even if I had, there'd be nothing to explain,' she said a little irritably. 'It wasn't as if you'd engineered the whole thing.'

There was instant mockery in the eyes that captured hers. 'How do you know I didn't?'

A pulse behaved idiotically in her throat, and a shadow of uncertainty was mirrored in the eyes she raised to his. 'Did you?'

His hand tightened on her shoulder and all at once his presence in the small cabin suggested a certain intimacy that made her heartbeats quicken erratically.

'I could have,' he suggested mockingly, his glance caressing the soft curves of her youthful body beneath the beige sweater and brown slacks.

His glance lingered until, heated and flustered,

she turned from him with a jerky movement, turning her back on the assault to her senses by his sheer masculinity. 'You wouldn't,' she said unsteadily. 'You wouldn't do that.'

'No, I wouldn't,' he stated harshly after a frightening little pause. 'For that kind of entertainment I prefer women with experience.'

The colour surged painfully into her cheeks and she was not sure whether she felt relieved or hurt by his remark, but, while they ate the meal she had prepared, she was more conscious of Kyle than ever before; conscious of his strength and vitality, and of her own vulnerability.

Kyle volunteered to make the coffee while she washed the dishes and stacked them away, and then he joined her on the wide bunk where they sat drinking their coffee in silence. His shoulder was disturbingly warm against her own, and she moved away slightly, adjusting her position with care so as not to evoke his mockery.

'I suppose your father will be wondering what's happened to you,' she said eventually in a frantic effort to break the lengthy silence between them.

'My father stopped wondering about me a long time ago,' Kyle announced dryly, taking her empty cup from her and placing it on the low cupboard beside his own. The movement brought him up against her, and she was suddenly conscious of that throbbing awareness between them; an awareness that made her tremble when she felt his hand beneath her chin as he forced her to meet his probing, tawny gaze. 'Are you afraid of being alone here with me?'

'N-no.'

'Liar,' he laughed softly, his fingers caressing her

throat and sending shivers of fire through her. 'You're an innocent baby where men are concerned, and you're scared stiff of what I might do to you.'

'I don't know what you mean,' she protested weakly, intoxicated now by his nearness.

'No, I don't suppose you do,' he muttered with a measure of impatience in his voice as he undid the pins in her hair so that it cascaded down her back in a dark, shining curtain. 'Perhaps this is as good a time as any to give you a lesson in love.'

She tried to move away, but his hands had twisted themselves about her hair, and unless she wanted to inflict pain upon herself, she was forced to remain still. His breath was warm against her cheek, then his mouth caressed the sensitive areas of her throat with devastating results before the tip of his tongue, exploring her ear, sent shivers of undulated excitement racing through her. It was the first time anything like this had happened to her, but before she could formulate some sort of defence in her mind, she was taken wholly into his arms, and her faint gasp died beneath his hard, demanding mouth. Her lips quivered responsively beneath his, and he forced them apart to explore her mouth with an intimacy that sent liquid fire racing through her veins. Her mind was in a whirl as she locked her arms about his strong neck, while the only clear thought that registered was the knowledge that she loved him and never wanted this moment to end.

His hands cupped her breasts beneath her sweater, awakening her to a tumult of sensations she had never experienced before, and then, quite suddenly, he was thrusting her from him with a savagery she could not understand.

'I wish to heaven I'd never met you,' his voice

grated harshly along her sensitive nerves.

Her lips quivered and her eyes filled with hot tears as she watched him stride towards the door. 'If I've done something wrong, then I—I'm sorry.'

'*You're* sorry?' he demanded harshly, and she shrank visibly from the fury in his eyes as he swung round to face her. 'I should never have invited you on board knowing how explosive the situation was between us.' He was leaning over her suddenly, pinning her down with his eyes, and making her frighteningly aware of the strange power he had over her. 'You can't say that you've been unaware of what's happening between us whenever we have met. You can feel it *now*, can't you?'

She tried to speak, but couldn't, and then the flame of passion in his eyes seemed to devour her. Her head was thrust back with the force of his mouth against her own, and then she felt herself being lowered on to the bunk. To resist never occurred to her, for nothing mattered except the pulsating joy of his hands on her untutored body. She knew that it was wrong to allow a man such intimacies, but with Kyle it seemed so right. Kyle was not just *any* man; he was the man she loved, and although she did not quite understand what was happening to her, she trusted him implicitly.

Drugged with love, she was only vaguely conscious of being undressed, and, in between caresses, Kyle pulled off his own sweater and shorts. An odd weakness invaded her limbs when she felt the hard length of his heated body against her own, and she clung to him rapturously as alien emotions stormed through her, shutting out everything except the desire to be closer to him still. She moaned softly, hardly aware of arching her body towards his, and then her arms were suddenly empty as he rolled away from her and swung his feet to the floor.

'God, I must be going mad!' he groaned, brushing an unsteady hand over his damp face.

'Kyle?' she questioned unsteadily, the husky note in her voice deepened with the feelings he had aroused, and, in her innocence, she reached for him. 'Don't be angry with me, Kyle.'

He seemed to shudder when she touched him. 'You're playing with fire,' he warned thickly, but, as he looked down on to her slender nakedness, a low growl emanated from deep within his throat, and he returned to her side, moulding her softness to the hard contours of his body.

The memory of that night still had the power to make Tricia cringe with shame. She blamed herself mostly for allowing the situation to develop that far, and, after so many years had elapsed, not even her plea of innocence salved her conscience any more.

Her body felt damp with perspiration as the memories forced their way back into her mind. She did not want to remember, but it was like trying to stop the flow of a raging river.

Her step had been light with happiness when she arrived at Benjamin Hammond's home the following afternoon. She had no doubt that she would see Kyle some time during the afternoon, and, humming softly to herself, she entered the house and made her way up the curved stairs to Benjamin's room.

To Tricia's dismay she found Benjamin involved in a violent argument with his stepdaughter.

Maxine was demanding a new, fast car to replace the Mini she had received on her last birthday, but Benjamin refused her the money, accusing her of being an unappreciative spendthrift. Tricia was quick to notice the change in his pallor. She tried desperately to intervene, but Maxine could not be stopped, and Benjamin finally suffered a seizure. He clutched at his chest with one hand, and reached with the other for the phial of tablets on the table beside his bed, but Maxine, a viciously evil glint in her green eyes, was there first, and Tricia looked on in horror as she held the phial beyond his reach.

'You can have your tablets if you promise to write out that cheque,' Maxine declared defiantly.

Tricia was too stunned initially to react, but one look at Benjamin's face made her lunge frantically at Maxine to wrest the phial from her hand, and rush to Benjamin's aid.

It was too late!

Benjamin was gone, and Tricia felt the coldness of his death like a mantle folding about her as she stared almost hypnotically down at his lifeless figure on the bed.

It was Maxine's screams that brought Kyle rushing up to his father's room, and she flung herself into her stepbrother's arms in a fit of uncontrollable hysteria when he had summed up the situation.

'It's *her* fault!' Maxine screamed repeatedly from the protective circle of Kyle's arms, and she pointed a slender, accusing finger at a bewildered, frightened Tricia. 'She wanted money, and Dad wouldn't give it to her. She refused to give him his tablets unless he wrote out a cheque for her, and now he's dead!'

A stricken look flashed across Tricia's face. She had known that Maxine disliked her, but she had never guessed how much until that moment. With the phial of tablets still clutched in her hand, like a stamp of guilt, she had no defence, but she could not let Maxine get away with twisting the truth so diabolically to her advantage.

It was then, however, that she recalled Benjamin once saying: 'Kyle has always idolised Maxine. She can never do wrong in his eyes, and he believes implicitly everything she tells him. He's blind and deaf to her faults, and it would shatter him completely to discover how often she twisted the truth to save her own, wretched skin. I've often wanted to make him aware of this, but then I never had the heart to do so.'

'Do *I* have the heart to disillusion him?' Tricia asked herself, her temples throbbing painfully as she stared up into those cold, accusing eyes above Maxine's bowed head; eyes that were filling so rapidly with hatred that she recoiled from it inwardly. Could she take her own happiness at the expense of Kyle's utter disillusionment in someone he had loved and trusted for so many years?

Caught in the trap of her love for him, she lapsed into a wretched silence; a silence that served as an admission of guilt as Kyle set Maxine aside to tower over Tricia like the silver, swooping falcon he had hung about her neck the day before.

'You rotten, scheming bitch! I knew what you were the moment I set eyes on you, and I was right. Get out of this house before I throw you out, and never set foot in it again!'

The bitter hatred in his voice, and in the rigid

contours of his white face, had sliced through Tricia, and her tender, fragile happiness lay shattered about her. The love they had shared was forgotten, and all that remained was the passion of his contempt, she realised through the red mist of pain that engulfed her as she walked from that house never to return.

Tricia grew up that day when she was forced to set aside the childish dreams she had woven about Kyle Hammond. Kyle could not prevent her from attending his father's funeral two days later, but it was then that the stark reality of Benjamin's death descended upon her, and, after everyone had left the graveside, Tricia remained, weeping silently beneath the cypress trees.

A few days later she was summoned to an attorney's office in town, and there, in the presence of a tight-lipped Kyle, she was informed of the twenty-thousand Rand which Benjamin Hammond had bequeathed to her in his will.

Speechless with shock and surprise, Tricia had stared at the thin, wiry old man seated behind the large desk, certain that he had made a mistake, but a slight movement beside her made her look up into the cold, tawny eyes of the man who made no secret now of the fact that he felt nothing but contempt for her, and all that he thought she stood for.

'You've got what you wanted after all. I hope you'll be happy now,' Kyle said cuttingly before walking out of the office, and out of her life.

Benjamin Hammond, in his kindness, and quite unknowingly, had branded her the gold-digger Kyle had always accused her of being, and, turning back to the astounded attorney, Tricia had said tritely:

'I don't want that money. Please give it back to Kyle Hammond and his stepsister, with my compliments.'

'I can't do that, Miss Meredith,' the attorney had stated flatly, quoting several legal reasons why her wish could not be carried out.

'Do with it what you please, then. I want none of it, and I never want to hear of it again,' Tricia had informed him, and, with her shoulders squared proudly, she had walked out of that warm, spacious office to brave the cold of that windy June morning.

She had had no idea then of the agony and the shame and humiliation she would suffer during the months directly after Kyle had sold the house and moved to his permanent home in Cape Town, and even now, six years later, the memory was too painful to recall. She had hoped, for her own sake, that she would never meet Kyle again, but now, after all this time, he was coming back into her life, and into a position where she would be entirely at his mercy.

It was an uncomfortable thought to know that her future was being placed into the hands of a man who loathed and despised her, but, if she did not want to be branded a coward as well as all the other uncomplimentary names he had flung at her, then she would have to stay and face Kyle Hammond regardless of the consequences.

The news that Union Timber was taking over Barrett's was common knowledge among the staff by the end of that week. Some took it in their stride, while others viewed the news with considerable trepidation. Union Timber had a reputation for paying high salaries, but it demanded an equally high standard of work from its skilled employees, and some of the mill-hands at Barrett's had worked themselves up into noteworthy positions over the years from a very low level of education. It was these men who were the most concerned about the take-over. Most of them had large families to support, and chances were that they would find themselves out of work as a result of their lack of proper qualifications.

Queues formed outside Charles Barrett's office, and he dealt with the worried employees individually, doing his best to reassure them, but Tricia knew as well as anyone else that the final decision would rest with Kyle Hammond, the shrewd, hard-bitten head of Union Timber.

Tricia had several qualms about her own position once Kyle knew that she was an employee of Barrett's, and she found herself caught up in the black cloud of uncertainty that hovered over everyone else.

'You're being silly,' Frank Carlson told her quite firmly when she voiced her uncertainties while making them coffee the Sunday evening. 'He can't dismiss anyone unless he finds their work unsatisfactory,' he added.

'If my services are not required he'll soon find a valid reason for paying me off,' she argued absently, hastening to explain. 'It's not myself I'm worried about, actually. I could always find work somewhere else, but there are some of those men in the mill who might not find it so easy.'

Frank clenched the stem of his pipe between his teeth and his dark brows drew together in a frown as he pulled out a chair and sat down at the scrubbed wooden table in her small kitchen. 'Do you think there's a possibility that Kyle Hammond might pay off some of the staff?'

Tricia shrugged slightly as she placed their cups of coffee on the table and sat down opposite him. 'It was never easy to predict Kyle's actions, so I wouldn't hazard a guess.'

'When does Barrett expect him to arrive?'

'Tomorrow.'

The word hovered over her like a threat as she looked up into those grey eyes regarding her so steadily.

'Are you still nervous of meeting him?' Frank asked quietly.

'A little,' she admitted, a wavery smile hovering about her wide mouth. 'It's like having to go to the dentist with toothache. Until you're seated in that chair you have no idea whether he intends to fill the tooth, or extract it.'

'You'll know tomorrow,' he stated calmly, his large, work-roughened hand clasping hers across the table.

'I'll know tomorrow,' she echoed, and a shiver of apprehension spiralled through her, leaving her tense and strangely uncommunicative in Frank's company.

Sensing her desire to be alone, Frank left soon afterwards, and Tricia rinsed the cups automatically before going to bed. She slept badly that night, and was up and dressed long before sunrise on that misty autumn morning in April.

She prepared herself a breakfast of toast and fruit juice, but it remained almost untouched on the table when she went through to her bedroom and sat down in front of her dressing-table mirror to do her make-up. She was no longer the gauche nineteen-year-old girl Kyle had known six years ago, but a self-assured woman of twenty-five who had known the hell of utter despair and disillusionment. Her long hair, the colour of a raven's wing, had been cut shorter to curl softly about her delicately moulded features, and the soft material of her leaf-green dress accentuated the gentle, alluring curve of breasts and hips. Her dark, winged eyebrows were arched above heavily-lashed golden-brown eyes, and, below the straight, tip-tilted nose, her mouth was full and soft, with just the faintest suggestion of passion in the curve of the upper lip.

Tricia was not attractive by the usual standards, but there was a certain beauty in the directness of those dark, expressive eyes, in the smoothness of her healthy, gently tanned skin, in the proud carriage of her head above her straight, slim shoulders, and in the faint huskiness of her well-modulated voice.

She applied lipstick carefully to her lips, and stared critically at herself for a moment. Being forced to accept someone else's guilt as her own had not been easy, and over the years she had grown a protective outer shell against the things that hurt most. Mentally, she had managed to cut the ties with the past, but physically . . .? Through the cloth of her dress her fingers sought the silver falcon on its chain about her neck. She had so often wanted to shed this one tangible link with the past, but something had always prevented her from doing so, and the silver falcon had remained as a reminder, perhaps, of her youthful folly in giving her heart and her body to a man who had had no use for it.

Driving to work in her small green Citroën some minutes later, Tricia tried to make herself believe that this was going to be a day like any other, but when she entered the office building the air of nervous expectancy that met her shattered her fragile game of pretence. The floors had never been polished so brightly, the offices had never been so tidy, and the unusual silence in the old building was broken only by the hiss of whispering, anxious voices. The only thing missing from this spotless, businesslike image was the red carpet of welcome, Tricia thought wryly as she stepped into the lift and pressed the button for the third floor, but she almost laughed out loud when the lift came to an abrupt halt between the second and third floors. This was the first bit of normality she had encountered since entering the building, and she felt almost relieved as she pumped the third floor button with her finger. The lift shuddered into motion once more, and carried her without further mishap up to the next floor.

In her small office everything looked gratifyingly familiar, and, removing the cover from her typewriter, she stared about her almost lovingly. She had spent many hours behind that desk typing Mr Barrett's correspondence, limiting the incoming calls, attending to the minor staff problems, and generally relieving her employer of the many little pressures that accompanied his position as head of the firm.

Tricia had a feeling that, as from today, nothing was going to be the same again; not with Kyle Hammand in charge of operations. She went through the usual ritual of sharpening her pencils and placing her notebook in readiness. Outwardly she appeared calm and composed, but inwardly every nerve-end seemed to be knotted so tightly that she wondered whether they would ever manage to unravel themselves again, and, as she glanced at the clock against the opposite wall, she knew that the moment she had dreaded would soon be upon her.

Footsteps approaching the office heralded Charles Barrett's arrival, but he was not alone by the sound of it, and moments later Tricia found herself confronting a very different Kyle Hammond from the one she had remembered. He seemed to be taller and leaner, and his silvery hair now gave the impression that he had gone prematurely grey. The perfectly chiselled mouth was drawn into a tight line as if it had forgotten how to smile, and he looked considerably older than his thirty-two years.

Those peculiar tawny eyes fastened themselves on to Tricia, but, except for a slight flicker of his eyelids, he showed not a trace of emotion as Charles Barrett said casually, 'You remember Tricia Meredith, of course.'

'Of course.'

The deep timbre of his voice struck a painful chord of her memory, and, endeavouring to overcome the tension and awkwardness of that moment, she held out her hand politely and said quietly, 'Hello Kyle.'

A hot wave of embarrassment surged into her cheeks when he ignored her hand and turned his back on her to address Charles. 'If you don't mind, there are a few things I would like to discuss with you before my men arrive.'

'Certainly,' Charles replied, glancing sympathetically at Tricia as she lowered her hand self-consciously to her side. 'Come this way.'

When the door into Charles Barrett's office closed behind them, Tricia was surprised to find that her palms were damp with perspiration, and her legs were shaking so violently beneath her that she was forced to sit down hastily behind her desk. She sat for a time with her head in her hands, but it took several seconds for her to realise that the pounding in her ears was the sound of her own labouring heartbeats. The first hurdle had been crossed, but Tricia knew that there would be other, more difficult hurdles to negotiate, and she would have to do so without any assistance from Kyle.

By tea time that morning the place was swarming with Union Timber men. Every aspect of the mill and its employees had to be investigated, and Kyle's accountants seemed to be everywhere, delving into books which dated from several years back up to the present.

'I've never had to answer so many questions in all my life,' Rosalie Usher, one of the girls in the accounts department, complained to Tricia when they met briefly in the passage later that day. 'It was like being screened by the Secret Service!'

Tricia had not quite known what was expected of her that day. Her office became a thoroughfare for strange men in city suits while she waded through the small pile of work on her desk, but for the rest of the day she found herself making endless cups of tea, and putting numerous calls through to Union Timber's offices in Cape Town until she felt like a tea girl-cum-telephone operator instead of a private secretary.

It was after five that afternoon when Charles Barrett's tired voice came over the intercom on her desk, and she jumped nervously.

'Do you have the Lockhart file there with you, Tricia?'

'Yes, Mr Barrett.'

'Bring it through, will you?'

Charles Barrett's office looked as if a tornado had struck it. There were files and papers everywhere, and Charles had a look of exhaustion in his wrinkled face as she handed him the file he had requested.

Tricia had avoided looking at Kyle all day, but now her eyes were drawn irresistibly to that lean, muscular figure in the chair she had occupied so often when taking dictation. His brown shoes were of expensive leather, and his grey suit was impeccably tailored, but a little tremor of shock rippled through her when her eyes finally clashed with his. He had been observing her as well, but with such a look of contempt in those pale eyes that she drew her breath in sharply and took a pace away from him, almost as if she expected him to leap out of his chair and strike her.

'You may go home now, Tricia,' Charles Barrett announced, and Tricia focussed her attention on him gladly.

'If you're certain there's nothing more I can do for you,' she began, but Charles interrupted her with a weary smile.

'Kyle and I are almost through here, but there's no reason for you to remain until we are.'

'Very well, Mr Barrett. I'll say goodnight, then.'

'Goodnight, Tricia.'

She risked a glance at Kyle, but his tanned face

had resumed the expressionless mask it had worn all day. 'Goodnight, Mr Hammond.'

She turned away, not expecting him to acknowledge her, but his impersonal, 'Goodnight, Miss Meredith,' reached her ears just as her hand touched the door handle. She hesitated momentarily, tempted to turn and face him, but she changed her mind, and the unconscious plea in her eyes went unnoticed.

The rest of the week was as chaotic as that first day for Tricia, and all the time she was aware of Kyle, silent and accusing in the background.

CHAPTER THREE

It was on the Friday, Charles Barrett's last day at the office before he retired officially from the firm his grandfather had established, that the staff presented him with a stinkwood chest which had been made with care and meticulously carved by the workmen in the factory. It was a sad occasion, and when Charles unobtrusively wiped away a tear, Tricia felt her own eyes fill with the tears she had been so determined to keep in check all day.

'Come and spend a weekend with us at the cottage as soon as we've settled in, Tricia,' Charles said when they had a few moments alone together in the office.

'I shall look forward to it.'

'And, Tricia . . .' He paused at the sound of Kyle's footsteps approaching the office and, gripping her hands tightly, said hastily, 'Take care of yourself.'

Kyle walked in at that moment and his expression became faintly sardonic when his eyes rested on their tightly clasped hands. Tricia had seen that expression before, and a perfectly innocent handclasp suddenly became something to be ashamed of.

'We'll see you this evening for dinner, Kyle?' Charles smiled, releasing Tricia's hands and completely unaware of the speculation his action had aroused as he collected his battered briefcase and prepared to leave.

'I'll be there at seven sharp.'

Tricia sat down behind her typewriter as Kyle accompanied Charles Barrett out of the building, and, for the first time since Kyle's arrival, she assessed the situation. With Kyle's men on their way back to Cape Town, and Charles Barrett leaving to go into a much needed retirement, Tricia felt as though she had suddenly been marooned on a remote island with her worst enemy as her only companion. She would now have to face Kyle alone, knowing that he had nothing but contempt for her, and that he despised her for what he imagined she had done. Despite everything she had suffered, she had never been able to make herself hate him and, even now, she could not blame him entirely for having eyed her with suspicion, and neither could she despise him for having accepted Maxine's explanation so readily under the circumstances. She had, however, come out of the situation a little wiser than before. She would never give her heart so easily again, and, if she did consider such an action, it would be to someone more deserving; someone like Frank Carlson.

'Contemplating your sins?'

Tricia looked up sharply to see Kyle leaning against the outer door with his arms crossed over his chest, and her heart leapt in a half-forgotten way at the sight of him, although she remained outwardly cool and unmoved. 'You would like to think that, wouldn't you?'

He straightened and smiled derisively as he pushed his hands into the pockets of his pants and came towards her. 'It would at least count in your favour if I knew that you possessed a conscience, but that would be hoping for too much from someone such as yourself.'

She drew a careful, steadying breath. 'If you intend to continue insulting me in this manner, then I might as well warn you that I shan't tolerate it.'

'I don't think you're in a position to say what you will or will not tolerate. *I'm* the one who'll have to tolerate *you*, and you might as well know right now that you're here on sufferance.' His jaw hardened, and those yellowish-brown eyes glittered ominously. 'And while we're on the subject, I usually prefer employing people on whom I can rely, and whom I can trust implicitly, and I don't think you belong in either of those categories.'

Tricia winced inwardly at the deliberate thrust, but not for anything in the world would she let him see that he had scored a hit. She raised her chin a little defiantly and met the onslaught of those compelling eyes with a bravado she was far from experiencing. 'If you're suggesting that I'm unreliable and not to be trusted, Mr Hammond, then——'

'I trusted you with my father once, and that proved to be a mistake I shall regret for the rest of my life,' he cut in ruthlessly, and she paled visibly as he leaned towards her over the desk, his attitude menacing. 'That isn't much of a recommendation, if you ask me,' he added harshly.

Tricia clenched and unclenched her hands beneath the desk in helpless frustration. It had been a mistake to think that she could stay on after Kyle had taken over from Charles Barrett, and for her sake, as well as Kyle's, it seemed best now that she should find employment elsewhere.

'I'll type out my resignation,' she announced quietly.

'I'm not asking for your resignation,' he snapped, his eyes frighteningly cold and hard as he took in her neat appearance. 'You're going to work, and work hard, for every cent you earn, and I want you to know that, from this moment onwards, I shall be watching everything you do or say. One wrong move, Tricia Meredith, and I shan't hesitate to send you packing. Not only that,' he added, and his voice had a sudden menacing ring to it that sent a chill up her spine, 'I'll make damn certain that no one else will employ you.'

Tricia experienced a multitude of emotions during the ensuing silence, but she could put a name to only three of them—fear, resentment, and anger. Fear, because Kyle had it in his power to do exactly as he had threatened; resentment, because of his unjust accusations; and anger at herself because of her sensitivity and inability to alter the situation.

It was anger, however, that came to her rescue, and she raised dark, stormy eyes to his as she said tritely, 'Was there anything else, Mr Hammond, sir?'

'Yes,' he replied curtly, his lips tightening into a thin, hard line of disapproval. 'Don't be insolent.'

He slammed the door of the inner office behind him with such violence that Tricia flinched visibly behind her typewriter as if she had been struck, and then, for some obscure reason, she wanted to laugh out loud, but she smothered the desire forcibly and tried to concentrate on the letters she still had to type before she could go home that afternoon to the safety and security of her small flat overlooking the lagoon.

With Frank away visiting his sister in George, Tricia spent a quiet weekend doing her shopping, seeing to her clothes, and generally tidying her flat. She tried not to think of her immediate future with Kyle temporarily at the helm of Barrett's, but her thoughts returned relentlessly to the subject, and she knew that she had no option but to bear Kyle's presence until he was ready to install someone from Union Timber into this new managerial position.

On the Sunday evening, while she made herself a sandwich, she thought of Kyle incessantly. As the years had flowed one into the other she had managed to limit herself to an occasional brief thought of him, but now he had suddenly come back into her life with a vengeance. He was beginning to dominate her thoughts once more, but she was determined not to allow him to dominate her very soul again. Over the years she had freed herself of the bonds of his personal magnetism, and she had no intention of falling captive to it again. She was cured, she told herself firmly as she bit into her chicken sandwich. She was cured of her childish infatuation for a man who had seemed to possess all the qualities her young heart had dreamed of, but disillusionment and cruel fate had shattered her girlish dreams, leaving her older and wiser, and wary of giving her heart again.

She finished her sandwich and drank her coffee, then deliberately rechanelled her thoughts to think of Frank. He was a dear, lovable man, and he wanted to marry her, but somehow she could never think of him as anything but a kind, dependable friend. As his wife she would feel secure in his love, but, with so little to offer in return, she had always shied away from the thought of marrying him.

She sighed suddenly, and, as her troubled glance rested on the pile of washing that still had to be ironed, she hurriedly washed her supper things and set up the ironing board.

She worked steadily for almost two hours, and it was after nine that evening when there was a knock at her door. Thinking that it was Frank who had managed to get back earlier than he had expected, she switched off the iron and pulled the plug out of the wall socket before answering the door.

'Kyle!' she exclaimed in mingled fear and astonishment, her heart leaping into her throat at the sight of the tall, silver-haired man standing on her doorstep.

'May I come in?'

'It's late,' she protested in a voice that sounded oddly strangled, but Kyle was already inside, a cynical smile curving that hard mouth as he stepped past her.

'It's never too late for old friends to call on each other, surely,' he replied in that smooth, deep voice of his as he stood regarding her closely in the small, dimly lit entrance hall.

Conscious suddenly of her faded cotton frock and shiny nose, Tricia led the way into her small lounge and contradicted him a little breathlessly. 'We were never friends.'

'That was because I saw through you from the start,' he hit back at her, but she chose to ignore his remark, and stood observing him nervously from a safe distance.

Seeing him daily in the office during the past week, she had been strangely detached and unmoved by his presence, but seeing him seated in one of the comfortable armchairs in her flat was a different matter entirely. His presence was now a threat to her personal privacy, and, as she took in the length of his lean, muscular frame clad in immaculate grey slacks and matching jacket, she was made incredibly aware of the magnetism he had always exuded. She was no longer a child of nineteen who was inexperienced and gullible. She was six years older and quite capable of withstanding him, she told herself firmly, but, as her wary eyes fastened themselves on to his dark blue shirt and strayed to where he had unbuttoned the collar to display the tanned column of his strong neck, she could almost feel the remembered texture of his skin against her own, and a familiar warmth surged into her limbs.

A film of perspiration broke out on her forehead and, angry with herself for still finding herself physically attracted to him, she turned her back on him and walked across to the window to stare out across the lagoon to where it lay shimmering serenely in the moonlight.

'Why have you come here this evening, Kyle?' she asked quietly, turning to face him again when she had managed to control herself sufficiently.

'Curiosity mainly,' he explained, his sweeping glance taking in every detail of her small flat. His derisive glance lingered on the old but comfortable chairs, the antique writing desk she had found one day in a second-hand shop, and the stinkwood dining-room table and chairs she had spent months saving up for. 'With the twenty-thousand Rand my father had left you, you could have afforded something better than this, but it didn't last very long in your hot little hands, did it? You couldn't wait to spend it, could you?' Kyle demanded harshly, but his unexpected attack somehow rendered her speechless. 'Well? Why don't you say something?'

'You have all the answers, Kyle,' she managed at last, her fingers digging into the padded back-rest of the chair she was leaning against for support.

'Do I?' Kyle persisted cynically, his tawny eyes capturing hers relentlessly. 'Why did you do it, Tricia?'

The question hung heavily in the air between them, but she dared not give him the answer he required. Instead she said: 'Whatever you may think of me, Kyle, I was fond of your father.'

'So fond of him that you killed him for the money he intended leaving you?'

Tricia felt as if he had struck her, and she paled visibly. 'I had no idea he would leave me anything,' she argued, but she saw the disbelief in his eyes and gestured helplessly with her hands. 'You may think what you like.'

'Damn you!' he exploded, leaping from his chair to face her from a few paces away, and with the light directly above him he looked suddenly very much older than his thirty-two years. 'It's not just a matter of thinking what I like,' his voice lashed her mercilessly. 'The evidence against you was pretty conclusive, I would say.'

'Yes, of course,' she admitted dully as every painful detail flashed before her eyes. 'Maxine saw it all, didn't she?'

'She's suffered sleepless nights ever since,' Kyle disclosed, and Tricia's tightly compressed lips curved into a cynical smile.

'I'm not surprised.'

'What's that supposed to mean?' he demanded angrily.

'Nothing,' she snapped, substantiating her remark hastily with, 'Maxine was always inclined to be highly strung.'

Kyle's eyes seemed to bore into hers with a force that made her quiver inwardly. 'You don't deny causing my father's death, then?'

For one brief moment Tricia toyed with the crazy idea of telling him the truth, but she rejected it fiercely the next instant, and pride made her say, 'Would there be any use my denying it when Maxine had been there to witness it all?'

'My God!' He bridged the gap between them so swiftly that he was upon her before she had time to formulate a way of escape, and one strong, lean hand was latched about her slender throat, the fingers exerting an unmistakable, deadly pressure as he told her, 'I could kill you!'

Tricia had no doubt, at that moment, that he meant every word he was saying, and her dark eyes were wide with fear as she stared up into his face so close to hers. It was distorted with rage and totally unrelenting. She tried to speak, but she could not force a sound past those steely fingers about her throat for a few seconds, and then they slackened mercifully, giving her the opportunity to draw air into her tortured lungs.

'Killing me wouldn't bring back your father, Kyle,' she whispered hoarsely, aware now of that hard, muscular body against her own, forcing her back against the back-rest of the chair, and holding her totally captive.

'Killing you wouldn't bring back my father,' he agreed harshly, 'but it would give me the greatest feeling of satisfaction to know that I've avenged his death.'

'Kyle, I didn't——!' She bit back the truth as it threatened to spill from her lips, and said lamely, 'It wasn't intentional.'

'It was deliberate and malicious, I would say.'

'Kyle . . .'

'And to think that I actually began to——' He sucked his breath in sharply, and his fingers fastened themselves on to her hair, sending a sharp pain shooting through her scalp as he hissed angrily through his teeth, 'Why the hell couldn't you have used that money my father left you for a trip to the other side of the world? Why did you have to come back into my life after all these years?'

Tricia could have told him that it was *he* who had come back into *her* life, but instead she found herself staring up at him in something between fascination and terror as the anger drained from him, leaving only naked desire in the eyes that took in every facet of her pale features before they lingered with purposeful intent on her soft, quivering mouth. His hand released her hair to move sensually down the hollow of her back as he moulded her body to his, and then desire, primitive and uncontrollable, surged through her like a tidal wave, sweeping aside pride and resentment to make her face the horrifying, undeniable truth. Her love for Kyle was not as dead as she had schooled herself to believe. It had merely lain dormant, waiting almost for this moment when life would be breathed into it once more to make it flame even brighter than before.

'Kyle ...' she groaned, making an abortive attempt to free herself, but even as she did so, her treacherous body melted against his.

'You were always a worthless little slut,' he accused harshly before his mouth descended on hers.

He kissed her wildly and passionately, with a hunger that kindled her own, and the years fell away, taking her back to those brief moments of ecstasy they had once shared. It was the memory of what she had suffered afterwards, however, that made her cling to her sanity, and with one quick twist of her body she freed herself from Kyle's arms.

They stood facing each other in abject silence, both equally pale and shattered by what had occurred, but Kyle was the first to collect himself, and he said gratingly, 'If your expecting an apology, then you might as well know that you're not going to get one.'

'Shall we put the incident down to a mental lapse on both sides, and leave it at that?' she countered swiftly, regaining her composure with agonising difficulty.

'Put it down to what you damn well please!'

'You hate and despise me, Kyle, but no more than I hate and despise you, so don't go away with the idea that I'm still harbouring some of that childish infatuation I once had for you.'

He smiled cynically. 'If it wasn't infatuation that made you return my kisses in the way you did, then how would you explain what happened between us?'

'There's no explanation for it when two people despise each other as much as we do,' she retorted bitterly, hating herself for being so weak.

Kyle's glance was an insult as it swept down the length of her and upwards again to meet her veiled eyes. 'We shall have to tolerate each other during office hours for a time, but it would perhaps be advisable if we stayed out of each other's way at other times.'

'I agree,' she said abruptly, her hands clenching at her sides as she tried to control their trembling.

Kyle hesitated, as if he wanted to add something, then his lips tightened, and he strode out of her flat, slamming the door behind him with unnecessary force.

From her small balcony a few moments later she saw him drive away at speed in his white Porsche, then she went indoors, shutting the glass door behind her, and attempting to shut out the memory of the emotions he had once again aroused in her; emotions she had thought never to experience again.

The attraction was still there, and it had been a revelation to her to discover that it was now stronger than ever, but between them lay six years of heartache, suffering and suspicion, and Kyle's staunch belief that she had caused his father's untimely death for the sake of her greed for money.

Tricia laughed suddenly, but her laughter bordered on hysteria as she realised the devastating truth. She could still have Kyle if she wanted him, but would a few hours of passion satisfy her in preference to a marriage of stability which was built on trust?

Even as she contemplated the idea she shrank

from it mentally. Once before she had trusted implicitly that he would not fail her, and she had suffered the humiliating consequences alone. No! She could not go through that hell again. Never!

Kyle called her into his office the Monday morning, and it was as if nothing of significance had happened between them the evening before. He was coldly remote, and a somewhat formidable stranger, but Tricia's pulses settled down to their normal pace as he waved a dictatorial hand towards the vacant chair on the opposite side of the desk.

'I have several letters to dictate,' he informed her once she was seated. 'You do have a diploma in shorthand, I take it?'

Tricia, usually slow to anger, found that she had to keep her temper in check as she looked up into those cold, calculating eyes. 'I do, yes.'

'Then shall we waste no more time and get down to it?'

'I'm ready whenever you are, Mr Hammond,' she announced coolly, opening her notebook and holding her pencil poised above the paper.

There was a brief, almost calculating pause before Kyle commenced his dictation, and suddenly she was left in no doubt as to his intentions. He was dictating so fast that it took almost a superhuman effort on her part to keep up with him, but she was determined not to let him have the satisfaction of hearing her ask him to repeat anything for her.

'Am I going too fast for you?' he asked at length with mock politeness.

'Not at all,' she replied acidly. 'I've always wanted to break the world record for speedwriting.'

Their glances clashed; and she could have sworn that she saw a flicker of humour in his pale eyes, but it was gone before it had taken actual shape as he continued dictating at a more reasonable pace.

'Bring those letters through to me for my signature the moment you've typed them,' Kyle instructed after almost an hour of dictation. 'I want them in the post as soon as possible.'

'I'll do that.'

'And here's something else,' he stopped her on her way to the door, and she turned to take the sheet of paper from him on which he had drawn up a list of names in his bold handwriting. 'I would like to see these men tomorrow. Make appointments for them to come up and see me individually.'

Tricit stared at the list apprehensively. 'How much time will you need with each one?'

'Not more than thirty minutes.'

She could no longer deny the suspicion that took shape in her mind and, throwing caution to the wind, she asked: 'Do you intend paying them off?'

Kyle's eyes narrowed perceptibly. 'I can't see that it's any business of yours, but it's quite likely that I shall have to.'

'Why?' she demanded boldly. 'Because they don't have the necessary papers to prove their qualifications?'

'Exactly,' he snapped, his expression forbidding. 'Now will you get out and do as I say?'

Tricia should have left it at that, but as she glanced down at the list of names she clutched in her hand, she knew that she could not leave the matter there. 'You can't do it, Kyle.'

'I beg your pardon?' he demanded with glacial

coldness, rising behind the desk to his full height and pinning her to the floor with those peculiar tawny eyes of his.

'You can't do it,' she repeated with a touch of defiance in the way she raised her chin. 'These men have been working for this firm for too many years to be treated this way. Their experience alone should count more than a governmental paper verifying their skill. And besides . . .' she swallowed nervously, 'many of them have large families to support. If you pay them off, then you might as well cut their throats.'

'No business can afford passengers,' Kyle explained harshly.

'Passengers?' she bit out the word incredulously, her usually warm brown eyes sparkling with anger. 'None of these men are passengers! They work hard for their money, and they deserve every cent they get, *and* more. What you're contemplating is nothing short of a criminal offence, and I shudder to think of the consequences. These are senior men,' she continued, waving the paper at him furiously. 'They're seniors in years and experience. Sack them, and you'll have a riot on your hands, and starving families on your conscience.'

'Have you quite finished?' Kyle's curiously controlled voice broke the deathly silence which had followed her outburst, and to her dismay, she found that she was shaking uncontrollably from head to foot.

'Yes, I'm finished.'

'Good,' he said abruptly. 'Now get out of here and do as you're told.'

She turned to leave, but at the door she hesitated,

glancing back at the tall, imposing figure behind the desk. 'Kyle ...'

His face darkened with fury. 'For God's sake, Tricia! If these men are as skilled as you say they are, and if they work as hard as you're trying to make me believe, then they won't have anything to fear tomorrow, will they?'

'I suppose not,' she agreed in a shaky voice, leaving his office and closing the door quietly behind her.

Tricia scanned through the list in her hand once more and set about making the appointments for the following day, but she did so with a heavy heart. As the head of Union Timber, Kyle could be totally ruthless in the face of suspected incompetence and inefficiency among his staff, and knowing this, Tricia could only hope and pray that these men would impress him sufficiently to make him realise their worth.

'This filing system is archaic,' Kyle complained later that morning when she took a batch of letters through to him for his signature, and found him fuming his way through the cabinets in search of a particular file.

'Mr Barrett had old-fashioned ideas, I know, but he was happy with it that way.'

'Well, I'm not,' Kyle exploded as she handed him the file he had been searching for. 'The entire filing system will have to be altered, and that will mean working several hours' overtime.' He shot a challenging glance at her. 'Any objections?'

If he had expected her to shy away from the amount of work involved in the task he envisaged, then she was determined to prove him wrong, she decided as she said stiffly, 'I have no objections at all, Mr Hammond.'

'Right,' he nodded abruptly, waving her into a chair while he glanced through the letters she had typed, and attached his signature to them.

Tricia sat there silently, her eyes drawn involuntarily to his strong, lean-fingered hands; clever, capable hands that could inflict pain as easily as they could arouse passion, and the ghost from the past reared its head, making her recall the far-reaching effects of that one regrettable occasion when she had been so completely at his mercy. Innocent, trusting, and willing in her eagerness to please the man she had secretly loved so much, she had followed blindly where he had led, never guessing that the path she had chosen would take her from the heights of undreamed-of ecstasy down to the very gates of hell.

'Get these letters in the post so that we can get started on the new filing system,' Kyle's authoritative voice cut across her disturbing line of thought, and she shuddered inwardly as she pulled herself together to carry out his instructions.

Afterwards there was no time for thoughts of any nature except those concerning work, and the day passed with a swiftness that eventually made her glance incredulously at the clock against the wall. It was six-thirty, and they were most probably the only people left in the office building, she realised to her dismay.

'I hope this hasn't made you late for an appointment,' Kyle remarked, reaching for his jacket and pulling it on, but there was not the slightest sign of concern in the eyes that met hers—only cold, hard cynicism.

'As if you really cared!' she flared angrily before she could prevent herself, and he mocked her openly now, fanning the fire of her anger.

'I always have the welfare of my employees at heart.'

'You don't possess a heart, Kyle,' she accused unwisely. 'You possess a computerised machine that does all the necessary things humans do, but you never programmed it in the art of caring.'

He was beside her in an instant, his eyes narrow slits of yellow fire in his taut face, and his hands bruising her shoulders as he lifted her almost bodily out of her chair. The swiftness with which he had moved was as unexpected as it was electrifying, and coming into contact with that lean, hard frame sparked off a succession of unwanted sensations that sent a dangerous weakness flowing into her limbs.

'You go too far, Tricia Meredith, when you presume to sit in judgment of my character, and most especially when yours is not as flawless as you would have others believe,' he said in that quietly ominous voice she knew so well, and his hands on her shoulders inflicted a punishment that was bruising as he warned darkly, 'Don't try me too far. You may live to regret it.'

Tricia remained perfectly still in his grasp, her body taut with the effort to control her wayward emotions, and then, surprisingly, she felt him tremble against her, and saw that odd little pulse jumping in his cheek. Her own pulse leapt in response, and she held her breath as he lowered his head purposefully, but the next moment she was being thrust from him with an exclamation of disgust on his lips.

'Go home!' he ordered harshly. 'Go home before I do something I know we both shall regret.'

Feeling peculiarly bereft, she turned and brushed past him without a word, but later, as she drove herself home, she despised herself for allowing him to affect her in the way he did. There was one small consolation, though, and that was the knowledge that Kyle was not as unaffected by her as he wished her to believe. She could perhaps play him at his own game, she thought cynically, but she had no doubt that she would once again be the one to suffer afterwards.

CHAPTER FOUR

TRICIA was in one of her rare moods when Frank came to see her at the flat later that evening, and, for the first time since knowing him, she wished he had stayed away. She was wrestling mentally with a bout of depression and listlessness, and somehow the conversation refused to flow.

'What's the matter, Tricia?' Frank demanded quietly after a lengthy, brooding silence had dominated her small lounge.

'Nothing's the matter,' she said evasively, avoiding his grey, searching gaze, and trying to concentrate on the knitting which had lain forgotten in her lap.

'You're looking a bit peaky, and you're not usually this silent,' he observed, smoking his pipe in thoughtful silence for a moment before asking, 'Are things getting a bit difficult at the office?'

Tricia stared at him for a moment, and realised that it was useless trying to hide things from him. He knew her too well to be fobbed off with evasive answers, and a tight little smile curved her lips as she said: 'A bit difficult, yes.'

'Is Kyle treating you badly?'

'No, I wouldn't say that. It's just——' She paused, chewing thoughtfully at her lower lip as she tried to find the right words to explain the situation. 'It isn't very easy trying to shut out the past when you find yourself face to face with it every day.'

'It's odd that he should have come to Knysna personally to attend to the take-over,' Frank remarked after yet another lengthy silence. 'One would have thought he would have sent one of his senior men instead.'

'Knowing Kyle, I don't find it strange at all,' she replied with a hint of sarcasm in her voice. 'He's arrogant enough to believe that no one else has the ability to attend to these matters successfully.' She met Frank's steady glance and felt suddenly ashamed of herself. 'No, that isn't strictly the truth.'

'What is the truth, then?'

Tricia put her knitting aside and got to her feet to pace the floor restlessly. She paused for a moment beside the window to stare out at the lights across the lagoon, and their rippling reflection in the water, and then, turning back to Frank, she said: 'In all fairness, Kyle was never the kind of man to sit back while others did the work, and since he's the chief director of Union Timber, it doesn't surprise me to discover that he should take such an active part in every project his company undertakes.'

'You make him sound quite human.'

'Oh, yes, he's human all right.' Her laugh was a little brittle as she added: 'But he's not very *humane* where I'm concerned.'

Frank frowned down at his pipe, and then, as she passed his chair, he caught hold of her wrist. 'Tricia ... don't let him hurt you again.'

Startled, she glanced down at him, and at the deep concern in those steady grey eyes she said firmly, 'I made a fool of myself once, and I don't intend to tread the same road a second time.'

A slow smile played across his craggy face. 'I'm happy to hear that.'

Tricia smiled back at him, but there was a peculiar tightness about her heart which she refused to analyse at that moment as she disengaged her hand from his. 'I'm going to make us something to drink, Frank, and then you must go. I have a heavy day ahead of me tomorrow, and I'd like to get to bed early.'

The tightness about her heart relaxed after Frank had gone and, as her own words returned to mock her, she found herself facing the shattering truth once again. 'I don't intend to tread the same road a second time,' she had said, but, like a fool, she was already treading that road. She had walked into the trap with her eyes open to be caught yet again.

The men Kyle had requested to see came and went in a steady stream all morning. Fear and uncertainty lined their faces as Tricia ushered them into Kyle's office and closed the door behind them, but, miraculously, they all emerged looking intensely relieved.

As Tricia saw the last of them out, she turned to find Kyle standing beside her desk, his eyes mockingly derisive as they flicked over her slim form, and she swallowed nervously.

'I take it they're staying?'

'They're staying,' he confirmed abruptly, and with that the matter was closed, but she could not help wondering afterwards whether her outburst had somehow had something to do with his decision.

'Don't be ridiculous! Kyle would never listen to

you!' she chided herself, and with that she brushed aside the incident.

As the week progressed Tricia had very little time to think of anything other than work, and not even the fact that she was working in such close proximity with Kyle seemed to disturb her. The complete re-organisation of the filing system took up most of her lunch hours, and necessitated an extra hour or two at least after five in the evenings. It seemed to be a mad week with lumber trucks coming and going at closer intervals, and production in the mill and the factory stepping up several paces. Surveyors roamed the grounds, architects fought over the sensibility of their plans for the new buildings to be erected, and an irate security guard had to be pacified when he complained about these unauthorised comings and goings.

'Transfer these documents into the new file, and sort them into date order,' Kyle instructed the Friday afternoon as they prepared to work through yet another lunch hour, and she almost hated him for looking so vitally energetic while she felt so absolutely drained of vitality. 'If we can get through this batch today then we're almost done,' he continued, but the telephone, which she had switched through to his office, rang shrilly on his desk. He answered it irritably, then extended the receiver towards her. 'It's for you.'

'Tricia Meredith speaking,' she said, frowning into the mouthpiece, but her brow cleared as Frank's voice came over the line.

'Hello, stranger. I haven't seen you all week, so what about meeting me for lunch somewhere today?'

'I'm afraid I can't,' she replied, aware of Kyle watching her intently as he sat back in his chair and lit a cigarette.

'Why not, for goodness' sake?' Frank demanded.

'Perhaps some other time?'

There was a pause, then Frank seemed to grasp the situation. 'I take it that Kyle's there in the office with you.'

Tricia sighed inwardly. 'That's right.'

'Is he making you work through your lunch hour?'

'Yes.'

'He sounds like a slave-driver.'

She suppressed a smile. 'Not really.'

'You're entitled to a lunch break, you know.'

'Yes, I know.'

'Well then, why don't you insist?' Frank demanded with a hint of irritation in his voice, and there was another pause as she remained silent, her lips sealed by the austere presence of the silver-haired man across the desk from her. 'Oh, all right,' Frank sighed at length, understanding her unusual reticence. 'I'll arrange for us to have dinner somewhere this evening. Will seven-thirty suit you?'

'I think so,' she said carefully.

'See you then.'

'Thank you, Frank,' she replied, and as the line went dead she replaced the receiver on its hook.

'Was that your ... boy-friend?' Kyle questioned cynically, the slight pause in his voice insinuating something that made her anger rise sharply.

'Frank Carlson is a very dear friend, but not in the sense you mean,' she answered coldly, meeting his tawny glance with a glint of defiance in her eyes.

'Have you known him long?'

'Several years.'

'I presume he has a large bank account,' Kyle concluded derisively, and she stiffened with distaste.

'I wouldn't know.'

'You must be slipping,' he mocked her ruthlessly. 'It's not like you to pick a dud.'

She winced inwardly. 'It's none of your business.'

'I agree,' he said abruptly, crushing his newly-lit cigarette into the ashtray. 'Get those documents filed, will you?'

Tricia was glad to get home that evening, and, with the prospect of a lazy weekend ahead of her, she felt lighthearted. After dining out with Frank that evening, she was late in getting up the Saturday morning to do her shopping, but on the Sunday morning she was up at the usual hour and, pulling on a knitted jacket over her thin sweater, she went for a long, bracing walk after breakfast.

The chilly autumn breeze whipped colour into her cheeks, and she drew the air deep into her lungs, throwing back her head as she did so to watch the clouds gathering in the sky. It would rain later that day unless the wind changed direction, she thought idly, pushing her hands into the pockets of her jacket and lowering her head against the growing strength of the breeze as she continued her walk.

Lost in thought, she did not see the white Porsche cruise past to come to an abrupt stop a few metres ahead of her, neither did she see the man who got out of it until she was practically on top of him.

'Kyle!' she gasped, her startled glance taking in the width of his shoulders beneath the silk sweater and leather jacket, and the long, muscular legs encased in faded denims. The wind had blown his hair across his wide forehead, making him look younger and less formidable, and seeing him like this jolted her memory painfully, but she thrust aside the mental vision of those hours she had once spent with him on his yacht when she saw his narrowed, tawny eyes roam with contemptible familiarity down the length of her, leaving her with the alarming sensation that she had been stripped systematically down to her skin.

Her body became heated despite the chill in the air as she withstood his probing, electrifying glances, but, when her senses began to respond wildly to the irresistible pull of his magnetism, she struggled mentally to free herself.

'What do we do now?' she demanded with forced flippancy, keeping in mind his suggestion that they should stay out of each other's way out of office hours. 'Do we look the other way and pretend we never saw each other?'

'It's too late for that,' he said abruptly, his expression inscrutable as he jerked open the car door. 'Get in.'

Tricia backed away from him. 'I don't think——'

'Get in!' he ordered sharply, but as she continued to shrink from him, he gripped her arm roughly and thrust her unceremoniously into the front seat before going round to the driver's side.

As he slid his tall frame into the seat beside her and turned the key in the ignition, she asked anxiously, 'Where are you taking me?'

'You'll find out soon enough,' was the only reply she received, and she decided against questioning

him further while he was in this mood of suppressed
fury.

Placing as much distance between them as the
interior of the car would allow, she stared out of the
window in silence, and tried desperately to still the
frightened beat of her heart. What was he up to?
she wondered nervously as they left the town behind
them, but when he turned off on to the road leading
up to Coney Glen, she felt a suffocating tightness
gripping her chest.

Kyle parked his car almost at the exact spot where
she had originally met his father, but the magnificent view of the lagoon with the backdrop of the
Outeniqua mountains was lost on Tricia as she felt
herself being submerged in a well of blind panic.

'Why did you bring me here?' she questioned
him in a voice that was tight and husky with fear.

'This was where it all started, wasn't it?' he demanded, sliding an arm along the back of the seat
as he turned to face her, and what she saw in his eyes
made her shrink even further from him.

'Kyle——'

'Wasn't it?' he persisted harshly.

'If you mean is this where I met your father, then
the answer is yes,' she replied stiffly, wrenching her
eyes from his compelling gaze to stare out beyond the
Heads towards the turbulent sea in an effort to control herself.

'Have you been up here since?' he questioned
her further.

'A few times.'

'In the hope of finding another rich old man who
might leave you a fortune in his will?'

She flinched as if he had struck her, then anger

came to her rescue, giving her the courage to face up to him. 'Did you bring me here to insult me, Kyle?'

'Did you think that I brought you up here to make love to you?' he demanded contemptuously as he gazed down into her stormy eyes.

'I've taken about as much as I can stand from you,' she cried hoarsely, fumbling for the door handle, but Kyle leaned over her, his hand gripping her wrist painfully as he prevented her from attempting to escape.

She felt his breath against her forehead, and the heat of his body so disturbingly close to hers. She fought against the hands that held her, then his arms were about her like steel bands trapping her against his hard, solid chest.

'I don't know why I was mad enough to bring you here,' he announced thickly, the pressure of his arms foiling her struggle for freedom. 'I'm beginning to suspect that you're a witch, because every time I come near you I no longer have the desire for anything else except this.'

His mouth swooped down on to hers to demonstrate his point, and her protests were silenced effectively while her lips were parted to draw a response from her she would have given anything to withhold. His hands slid inside her jacket and up beneath her sweater to cup her breasts with a familiar expertise, those lean fingers probing, caressing, until a shudder of ecstasy shook through her.

'Kyle!' she gasped his name, half in protest, half in delight, but as her fingers entwined themselves in his hair, he took her roughly by the wrists and thrust her from him so that she fell back dazedly against the door.

His face had gone peculiarly white beneath his tan, and the hands which had caressed her a moment ago were now gripping the steering wheel so tightly that she almost feared it would snap. 'I despise you, Tricia Meredith. But I despise myself more for still finding you desirable.'

'Is that so terrible?' she asked shakily, trying to suppress the tumult of emotions he had aroused in her, and no longer entirely convinced that he despised her as much as he was trying to make her believe.

'After what you did to my father?' he demanded harshly as he turned in his seat, his eyes cold and hard as they raked over her. 'I should have had you slapped into prison, but Maxine pleaded with me not to.'

Naturally Maxine would have prevented him from doing any such thing, she thought with a touch of cynicism, and laughing a little hysterically, she said: 'How ... very kind of her.'

'Stop that at once!' his voice lashed her, and she sobered instantly.

'I'm sorry.'

'I fail to see what you found so amusing,' he continued in that bitingly cold voice that sent an involuntary shiver up her spine. 'Maxine is a very gentle and sensitive-natured person.'

'Oh, I'm sure she is.'

'This is not the first time you have adopted a sarcastic attitude when discussing Maxine,' he observed thoughtfully, his eyes narrowed and watchful as they probed hers. 'You resent the fact that she witnessed the scene that caused my father's death, don't you?'

They were treading on dangerous ground, and she was instantly on the alert. 'I don't resent Maxine at all.'

'You should be grateful to her.'

'Should I?' she asked with a hint of cynicism in her voice, but the eyes she raised to his were curious. 'Would you really have gone to the police?'

His lips tightened cruelly. 'I considered it.'

'And Maxine talked you out of it,' she concluded softly, fighting against the pain deep down inside of her.

'Maxine is a very forgiving person, and if you'd taken the trouble to get to know her, you would have known that.'

'Did *you* ever take the trouble to really get to know *me*?' she countered swiftly in annoyance.

'I saw through you from the very first moment we met.'

She winced inwardly and stared out across the lagoon to where the yachts were making the most of the wind, then she said bitterly, 'You saw only what your suspicious mind wanted to see.'

'I was right to be suspicious of you, wasn't I.'

It was a statement, not a question which could have indicated a certain element of doubt, but Tricia parried the thrust bravely by saying, 'There was a time when you felt a little differently about me.'

'I was a fool to allow myself to be swayed by your practised look of innocence,' he said bitingly, his expression hard and cynical as he faced her. 'You fooled my father, and you finally fooled me—but not for long. You were after money, and you made sure you got it, didn't you!'

The desire to explain was very strong, and although she could not divulge the truth about that one very important factor, she could at least try to make him understand the innocence of her relationship with his father.

'I had your father's friendship, Kyle, and that was enough for me. I loved him like the father I never had, and whether you believe me or not, I never had any idea that he intended leaving me anything in his will. If I had known, I would have rejected the idea strongly.' There was an unconscious note of pleading in her voice, and a look of utter sincerity in her warm brown eyes, but Kyle was blind to everything except his prejudiced beliefs. 'I met your father quite by accident,' she continued, staring out across the turbulent waters of the lagoon towards the hazy blue outline of the Outeniqua mountains in the distance. 'He needed help, and I gave it to him. We talked a lot that day while we sat up here waiting for his tablets to take complete effect, and your father somehow sensed my loneliness at the time, and my desperate need to belong somewhere.' Her eyes were misty with remembrance as she turned slightly in her seat to face the man who sat watching her so silently. 'I didn't want his money, Kyle, but it meant the world to me that your father was kind enough to make me feel occasionally that his home was mine, and that I belonged.'

There was an emotional little silence, then Kyle laughed cynically. 'That was a very pretty speech. How long did it take you to rehearse it?'

He possessed all the weapons to hurt her, and he wielded them satanically, while she was defenceless without the means to prove him wrong.

'I pity you, Kyle,' she said bitterly, torn between resentment and anger. 'You wouldn't recognise sincerity even if it was flashed in big bold letters on a screen in front of your very eyes. How dreadful it must be to live with the fear that there must always be an ulterior motive for someone offering their friendship.'

'It's people like you who've made me that way,' he parried harshly, and, driven beyond her limit, she raised her hand to strike him.

Her wrist was caught in mid-air, and her arm was twisted sharply, wringing a cry of pain from her lips which was stifled by the hard pressure of his mouth. His kiss was a punishment from which there was no escape, and she could offer no resistance to the forcefulness of his embrace. He released her and she numbly explored her bruised lower lip with the tip of her tongue, unaware of the provocativeness of her action until Kyle's swift indrawn breath made her raise her glance. Anger had been replaced by desire in those narrowed, tawny eyes, and his heartbeats quickened beneath her hands, but even as her pulses clamoured in response, he thrust her from him and started the car.

Bewildered and hurt, she shrank into the corner of her seat, and a stormy silence prevailed during the drive back to town. When he finally parked the car at the entrance to the building where she lived, Tricia turned in her seat to face him and raised her hands palm upwards in an apologetic, pleading gesture.

'Kyle...'

'I didn't know you charged for kisses and a little
light lovemaking,' he remarked cynically when she
paused in her search for the right words, and the
next moment a role of banknotes was thrust into her
hands.

Tricia stared at it stupidly for a moment, unable
to grasp the situation, then the blood drained from
her cheeks to leave her deathly pale. He had deliberately misunderstood her, and a strangled cry
seemed to come from the depths of her soul when
she dropped the money on the seat between them
as if it were a burning coal of fire and, wrenching
open the door, fled from him.

She was quivering with rage and humiliation
when she entered her flat and threw her keys down
on to the small table in the entrance hall. She tried
to shake off Kyle's insult, but her efforts were futile,
and every time she thought of it, it made her feel
cheap and dirty. She paced the confined floor space
of her lounge, trying to rid herself of the aching
misery which seemed to enfold her, but her actions
brought her no relief. She was a fool to care so much,
and an even bigger fool to have allowed herself to be
enveigled into a position where he could insult her
in this manner.

The doorbell rang sharply, interrupting her
thoughts, and jarring her already shattered nerves.
Caught in a paralysing grip of fear that it might be
Kyle who had followed her up, she stood rooted to
the floor, but when the doorbell rang a little more
urgently the second time, she managed to pull herself together sufficiently to answer it.

'I was beginning to think you were out,' Frank

remarked as she opened the door hesitantly, and she almost cried with relief as she stared up into those smiling grey eyes.

'Frank! Oh, Frank, it's wonderful to see you,' she exclaimed, clutching his arm and literally dragging him inside. 'I can do with the company of someone as sane and sensible as yourself.'

He pushed a hand through his unruly dark hair and eyed her with a measure of uncertainty. 'I'm not sure whether I should take that as a compliment or not.'

'Believe me, it was meant as a compliment,' she assured him adamantly as she took him through to the lounge. 'I've never before known anyone as warped and twisted as Kyle Hammond, nor anyone who could make such vile insinuations and accusations. I——' Her voice broke and she buried her quivering face in her hands, forcibly checking the tears which threatened to overflow. 'I wish I were dead,' she added in a muffled voice.

Strong arms were wrapped about her shaking form. 'Take in easy, Tricia, and tell me what brought this on.'

'I went out for a walk this morning and met Kyle quite by chance.' She raised her head from its resting place on his broad, comforting shoulder and lifted tear-filled eyes to his. 'Frank . . . what am I going to do?'

He was silent for a moment, his fingers gently brushing the soft, dark curls from her smooth forehead, then he kissed her lightly on her quivering lips and drew her down on to the sofa.

'Marry me, my dear,' he suggested with quiet sincerity, holding her hands captive against his chest.

'Let me protect you, and take care of you, then you never need be afraid again.'

'Oh, Frank ...' she sighed unsteadily, 'it won't work.'

'How can you be so sure of that?'

She shook her head slowly and bit her lip to steady it. 'You're a wonderful man, and a very dear friend, but marriage—marriage requires much more than that.'

'Tricia——'

'No—please,' she interrupted, and at the look of pain in his eyes she leaned forward impulsively and pressed her lips to his rough cheek. 'I'm sorry.'

'It's still Kyle, isn't it?' Tricia winced inwardly, but before she could reply he added abruptly, 'You don't have to say anything. I understand.'

Unable to look him in the eyes, she drew her hands from his and left him seated on the sofa to walk across to the window where she stood for a moment watching the angry clouds chasing each other across the sky, then she turned and said fiercely, 'I despise myself!'

Frank took out his pipe and filled it with characteristic thoroughness before he lit it and said: 'Why don't you tell him the truth?'

She dropped her gaze to the floor once more and shook her head. 'He wouldn't believe me.'

'Have you given it a try?'

'If he refuses to believe that I wanted nothing from his father other than his friendship, then he'll never believe that it was Maxine and not I who——' She broke off abruptly and steadied her quivering lip between her teeth. 'Oh, let's just forget it.'

'Would you like me to talk to him?'

'No!' she cried out sharply in fright, then, lowering her voice, she made herself say calmly, 'Kyle will want proof of my innocence, and I have none. It's my word against Maxine's, and he's always believed in her blindly.'

Frank blew a cloud of smoke into the air and scowled angrily. 'If I could get my hands on that young lady, I'd wring her neck!'

'And do away with the only person who could prove my innocence?' she laughed unsteadily, gradually regaining her equilibrium and her sense of humour.

'She will never do that, and you know it,' Frank retorted sharply.

No, Tricia thought, Maxine would never willingly tell the truth, and the realisation filled her with utter despondency. There was nothing she could do to alter the situation while Maxine chose to remain silent.

'I'll make us a pot of strong tea,' she said eventually, but as she passed Frank he roused himself from his thoughts.

'I'll always be there if you should need me, Tricia,' he said simply, and, as always, his sincerity touched her deeply.

'I know,' she smiled warmly, placing a light hand on his arm. 'And thank you.'

Frank stayed for tea, and later for lunch. She was more than grateful for his calming presence, and when he finally left she found that her nerves had unravelled themselves into a semblance of normality. She could now view her encounter with Kyle objectively, and without suffering too much, but it was still a subject she tried to avoid thinking about.

The rain came down in a torrent later that afternoon, and the downpour continued throughout the night. It was still raining when Tricia drove to work the following morning, and there was no sign that it might clear up during the day. She discarded her raincoat when she reached her office, and grimaced slightly when she felt the dampness of raindrops on her hair, but, as she hastily inspected her appearance in the mirror of her powder compact, she became aware of someone watching her.

Turning, she found Kyle observing her with a sardonic gleam in his tawny eyes, and her heart lurched uncomfortably at the sight of him. His silvery fair hair contrasted heavily with his tanned complexion and expensive dark suit which had been impeccably tailored to fit his lean, muscular body, but, as she felt the familiar stirring of her senses, she squared her shoulders and met his glance coolly.

'Good morning, Mr Hammond,' she greeted him with formal politeness, but with a hint of defiance in her voice.

'Get your notebook and pencil ready and come through to my office,' he ordered abruptly without returning her greeting, and several little devils were released simultaneously within her.

'Please,' she said distinctly.

Kyle turned, his heavy eyebrows raised above faintly incredulous eyes. 'I beg your pardon?'

'I merely added "please" to your command,' she explained with a calmness that amazed even herself. 'It's a strain working together, I know, but we could at least be polite to each other.'

'Really?'

'Sarcasm won't relieve the situation either,' she insisted with growing irritation. 'With Mr Barrett no longer here you happen to need me, and that's all there is to it.'

'You consider yourself indispensable?'

'For the next week or two, yes,' she insisted, and the brief silence that followed was electrifying.

'I must hand it to you, Tricia. You've certainly got nerve, if nothing else,' he laughed shortly, his mouth twisting with cynical humour. 'Don't you realise that you're risking instant dismissal?'

'Dismiss me if you wish, Mr Hammond, but are you prepared to spend treble the time accomplishing the changes you have in mind?' she asked a little daringly.

His eyes flickered dangerously. 'So you think you have me over the proverbial barrel, do you?'

'I don't like this any more than you do, Kyle, but . . .' She hesitated, realising for the first time that she might perhaps have gone too far, and she added quietly, 'Civility costs nothing, but on the other hand it achieves so much.'

'And what do you hope to achieve?' he hit back with calculating hardness. 'A double cheque at the end of the month?'

'Must you always bring money into it?' she demanded, anger overriding the hurt.

'Money is the only commodity that's ever been of any importance to you,' he replied, and his voice was now as cold as his eyes. 'You even killed for it.'

'Don't say that!' she gasped hoarsely, the colour draining from her face until her eyes were like two dark pools of pain, but Kyle showed her no mercy.

'Why not?' he demanded, his jaw rigid and unrelenting. 'It's the truth, and you can't deny it!'

'I could deny it, but what would be the use?' she thought miserably, but aloud she said: 'You certainly know how to strike hard where it hurts most.'

His glance seemed to soften for a moment as it rested on her quivering lips, then his expression hardened once more, and he said callously, 'You have only yourself to blame for that.'

'No, I'm not entirely to blame for it,' she contradicted absently, thinking of that afternoon when she had found Maxine in Benjamin's room. 'Circumstances placed me in the wrong place at the wrong time, and I——'

'Yes?' he prompted when she halted abruptly. 'You what?'

Horrified at how close she had come to revealing the truth, she said sharply, 'I wish we'd never met!'

'I echo that most heartily,' he snapped harshly, turning from her. 'There's work to be done. Come through to my office ...' He paused in the doorway, his mouth twisting cynically as he added: 'Please.'

She drew a careful, steadying breath, and muttered, 'Certainly, Mr Hammond.'

For the next hour or more, Tricia had no time to brood over their confrontation. Kyle dictated rapidly, and she had to keep her wits about her if she did not want to lag behind with her shorthand notes.

'I want to go through the personal files this morning. See to it that I'm not disturbed,' Kyle ordered when she finally closed her notebook, and once again he added cynically, 'Please.'

Tricia chose to ignore it, and sighed with relief when she closed the door between their offices and sat down behind her typewriter. The day had started wrong, and heaven only knew how it would end, she thought unhappily as she fed typing paper and carbon into her machine and flicked open her notebook.

CHAPTER FIVE

THE hours seemed to fly past that morning and, with only a short break for tea, Tricia worked on steadily. It was not until the letters she had typed were stacked in a neat pile on her desk that she started on the files which had to be re-sorted, and through it all she found herself dealing automatically with the incoming calls, taking down messages, and occasionally handing out the required information.

It was a few minutes to twelve when the telephone rang again and, raising the receiver to her ear, she said unsuspectingly, 'Mr Hammond's office, good morning.'

'I'd like to speak to Mr Hammond, please.'

Tricia almost dropped the receiver when she recognised Maxine's high-pitched voice, and, with her heart pounding uncomfortably in her throat, she said: 'I'm afraid Mr Hammond doesn't want to be disturbed at the moment.'

'He'll speak to me,' Maxine insisted sweetly, and apparently unaware of whom she was speaking to. 'Just tell him it's Maxine, and that it's important.'

Tricia hesitated only briefly before she flicked the required switches on her desk, and moments later Kyle's voice exploded in her ear.

'I thought I told you I didn't want to be disturbed!'

'I have Maxine on the line for you,' she said

apologetically. 'And she says it's important.'

'Blast!' he muttered with obvious irritation. 'Put her through, will you.'

Tricia did as he requested, and waited only long enough to hear Maxine's 'Kyle, *darling!*' before she replaced the receiver and tried to concentrate on her work once more.

It had shaken her considerably to hear Maxine's voice on the telephone, and her hands were trembling when she rearranged the papers into date order before placing them into the new files. The past was suddenly all around her, so suffocatingly and threateningly close that she wanted to scream, but she controlled herself with a visible effort and fought against the painful, haunting memory of that high-pitched voice accusing her of killing Benjamin Hammond.

Frank's telephone call some minutes later, inviting her to have dinner with him that evening, came as a welcome diversion from her thoughts, and she was in complete control of herself again when Kyle eventually emerged from his office an hour later.

'I have to go out,' he announced with a scowl on his lean face. 'Take an hour for lunch, but be back at two sharp so we can get on with those files.'

He was striding from the office before Tricia could reply, but she had no doubt that she had Maxine to thank for this unexpected reprieve from work, and, putting on her coat, she went out to buy herself something to eat at the snack-bar not far from the mill.

Kyle returned to the office after lunch in a thundering mood, and more than once that afternoon she found herself subjected unnecessarily to the sharp lash of his tongue. She eventually came to the conclusion that something must have happened between him and Maxine to upset him, and that in itself was odd, for an angry word had seldom ever passed between them as far as Tricia could remember.

She hastily brushed aside her thoughts when she saw Kyle directing a furious glance at her, and after that she concentrated solely on her work, but she was more than ordinarily relieved when it was finally time to pack up and go home.

That night, in the small, exclusive restaurant with its log cabin atmosphere, Tricia smiled at Frank across the candlelit table. They had been served with excellent seafood and wine, and she felt replenished and totally relaxed for the first time that day. It was a strain working so closely with Kyle every day, and it was becoming increasingly difficult to have to fight against the hopeless yearning for something she could never have; his trust, his respect . . . and his love!

'You're looking extremely beautiful this evening,' Frank's voice cut across her thoughts, and she flushed a little guiltily beneath the warmth of his glance as he added, 'I know I'm the envy of every man in this restaurant.'

Her eyes sparkled with laughter. 'You've said that before, and I don't believe you.'

'Am I repeating myself?' he asked, looking mildly surprised.

'You are,' she admitted, the corners of her mouth quivering with the effort not to smile. 'I don't mind, though. It's good for my morale.'

His glance was faintly reproving. 'You're laughing at me.'

'Yes,' she admitted, smiling openly now. 'But not in a nasty way.'

'I should hope not!'

'Have I ever been nasty to you?' she asked now with a tiny measure of uncertainty in her voice.

'If you have, then you've naturally been forgiven,' he remarked dryly, but the laughter in his eyes matched her own.

'I'm not quite sure what I should make of that remark, but thank you all the same,' she replied with an amused smile lifting the corners of her mouth.

Frank's hand found hers across the table as their eyes met and held, but his glance went beyond her suddenly, and she felt the pressure of his fingers increase about her own.

'Don't look now,' he warned softly, 'but Kyle Hammond has just entered the restaurant with a ravishing young lady on his arm. She looks as though she could be more at home in a fashion magazine.'

Tricia felt her back stiffen automatically as she waited a few seconds before turning her head casually in the direction of Frank's glance, and it was with a peculiar sense of relief that she recognised Kyle's stepsister. At twenty-four a year younger than Tricia, Maxine was stunningly beautiful. Her titian hair was piled high on her head in a sophisticated style, and her tall, slender body was clad in cream silk, Tricia noticed as Maxine removed her evening coat and slid gracefully into her alcove seat.

'That's Kyle's sister Maxine,' she explained absently to Frank while she marvelled silently at how attractive Maxine had become. 'She's a model.'

'One wouldn't say they're related, judging by the way she's behaving,' Frank remarked casually, and Tricia forced herself to look away from those two arresting figures seated at the other end of the restaurant.

'They're stepbrother and sister, actually.'

'Ah, that explains it.'

'Explains what?'

'They're not blood relations.'

'No.' She frowned down at the white tablecloth and twirled the stem of her empty wine glass between her restless fingers. 'Benjamin Hammond married Maxine's mother when Maxine was only a few years old, and Gloria Hammond died of leukaemia five years after their marriage.'

'Then, if I'm not entirely mistaken, there's nothing to stop the young lady from getting what she wants.'

Tricia stared at him blankly, sunk too deep in her own turbulent thoughts to grasp fully what he was saying. 'I'm sorry, Frank, I don't quite——'

'You're suddenly being extraordinarily dense, Tricia,' he accused with an exasperated sigh.

'I'm sorry,' she said again, pulling herself together and giving him her undivided attention this time despite the fact that she was aware of Kyle's presence with every fibre of her being. 'What is it you're trying to say?'

'Kyle Hammond and Maxine are not related to each other,' Frank explained with remarkable tolerance. 'In other words, if Maxine wishes, she could marry Kyle, and *vice versa*.'

'Maxine has always been a little possessive where

Kyle is concerned, and he's always adored her absolutely. But marriage?' She discarded the idea with a measure of distaste. 'No, I don't think Kyle——'

'Tricia,' Frank interrupted gently, 'I'm not suggesting that there's anything between them, and I'm not suggesting that Kyle has any intention of marrying his stepsister, but Maxine is certainly behaving in an extremely provocative manner towards someone who's supposed to be her brother, and if he adores her as much as you say, then there's nothing to stop them from marrying each other if Kyle is lured sufficiently to take the bait.'

Tricia considered this for a moment, admitting to herself that there was some truth in Frank's statement, but then she rejected the idea almost forcibly. Over the heads of the other diners she caught a glimpse of Maxine leaning towards Kyle with her head thrown back to expose the provocative curve from her slender neck down to the partially exposed fullness of her breasts. Her crimson lips were parted invitingly, and Kyle was staring at her with the intensity of a man totally bewitched.

A wave of nausea swept through Tricia, and she feared for a moment that she was about to embarrass Frank by being physically sick in public, but she swallowed convulsively, and forced down the nausea only to find that she was caught in the web of the most violent attack of jealousy she had ever experienced.

'I think I'd like to go home, if you don't mind,' she managed jerkily, and Frank signalled the waiter at once to settle the account.

With his hand firmly beneath her elbow she felt oddly secure, but, as they passed close to the alcove table, Kyle and Maxine looked up simultaneously. Kyle's features remained inscrutable as he inclined his head in a gesture of recognition, but Maxine seem to grow pale when her green eyes met Tricia's in passing.

Tricia shivered in the car as she relived that moment of coming face to face with Maxine. During that brief moment, when their eyes had met, Maxine's glance had registered surprise and a hint of fear before she had looked away. Was it possible that, now that Maxine was older, she might have regrets about what she had done? Tricia discarded the possibility with a touch of cynicism. The mere fact that Kyle was as yet unaware of the truth was enough proof that Maxine had not changed over the years.

'I'm sorry if I've upset you, my dear,' Frank broke the silence between them when she eventually unlocked the door to her flat and stepped inside. 'I was merely supposing——'

'I know,' she interrupted him gently, drawing him inside and closing the door. 'I'll make up a cup of coffee, shall I?'

She did not wait for him to answer, and, dropping her wrap and purse on to a chair, she went through to the kitchen to switch on the kettle. Frank followed her more slowly and stood just inside the door, watching her move about with a brooding expression on his face.

'The evening has been spoiled somehow, hasn't it?' he said at last when she carried their coffee through to the lounge.

'Not entirely,' she contradicted, smiling at him with her usual warmth. 'I must thank you for a superb dinner.'

Frank brushed aside her thanks with a careless wave of his hand, and, despite her attempts at light-hearted conversation while they drank their coffee, his mood remained thoughtful. She had never seen him like this before; brooding, almost moody, and it perturbed her to think that she had indirectly been the cause of it. When he finally placed his cup in the tray and announced that it was time he left, Tricia accompanied him in silence to the door. In the small, dimly lit entrance hall they stood for a moment facing each other. Her glance was wary, but his was intense and searching, and then he grunted something unintelligible as he locked his arms about her and found her lips with his own.

This was not the first time he had ever kissed her, but never before had he kissed her with such a fierce despair that made her feel slightly sick at her own inability to respond.

'Forgive me, Tricia,' he grunted again when he finally released her, and she almost felt his pain as acutely as if it were her own.

'There's nothing to forgive,' she tried to reassure him while his fingers lightly traced the tender curve from her cheek to her chin.

'When do I see you again?' he asked.

'I might meet you for lunch somewhere during the week, but give me a ring to confirm that, will you?'

'I'll do that,' he replied evenly, in complete control of himself now as he took her hand in his and raised it to his lips. 'Goodnight, my dear.'

She locked the door behind his departing figure and leaned tiredly against it for a moment before she put out the lights and went through to her room. She did not want to remember the desperation of

Frank's kiss, and she did not want to dwell on his distasteful suppositions concerning Kyle and Maxine, so, for the first time in some years, she swallowed down a sleeping tablet and went to bed.

Taking that tablet had been a mistake. When her alarm went off the following morning she found she was not yet ready to face the world, and as a result she arrived at the office looking heavy-eyed, as well as having to nurse a throbbing headache.

'Hangover?' Kyle queried abruptly when he found her swallowing down a couple of aspirins later that morning.

'A headache,' she explained with equal abruptness.

'You must have had a hectic night.'

Determined not to be riled by him, she said evenly, 'Not more hectic than your own, I'm sure.'

One fair eyebrow rose in sardonic amusement. 'I spent the best part of my evening with Maxine, and she's my stepsister ... remember?'

'I'm not likely to forget that,' she stated bluntly. 'Have you?'

His glance sharpened. 'What's that supposed to mean?'

'Nothing,' she snapped, despising herself for voicing the suspicions Frank had sown in her mind the previous evening.

'Tricia——'

The shrill ring of the telephone on her desk interrupted whatever he had been about to say, and she lifted the receiver thankfully.

'Mr Hammond's office ... Just a moment.' She placed her hand carefully over the mouthpiece and raised her eyes to meet Kyle's furious glance. 'A

Mr Snell from the Oceanic Shipping Company wishes to speak to you. Will you take the call in your office?'

'Put it through,' he ordered harshly, and, when the inner door closed behind him, a shiver of relief rippled through Tricia.

She would have to watch her step, she decided grimly when her heartbeats settled down to normality. To antagonise Kyle could only increase her suffering without leaving so much as a dent in his armour.

Her headache subsided gradually, but the telephone rang at regular intervals during that morning, and each time she found herself wincing inwardly at the stab of pain that shot through her temples. She was taking a well-earned break with a cup of tea when it rang again, and, suppressing her growing irritation, she lifted the receiver.

'Tricia?' a familiar voice purred into her ear before adding unnecessarily, 'This is Maxine.'

'I'll put you through to Kyle.'

'No, *wait!*' Maxine's anxious voice halted her in the process of putting the call through, and she waited tensely, her fingers hovering above the switches. 'It's you I wanted to talk to.'

'Oh?'

'I wondered if you could possibly spare the time to have lunch with me today?'

Tricia was instantly on the alert, and her hand tightened on the receiver until her knuckles showed white through the skin. 'May I know the reason for this invitation?'

'No specific reason, actually,' Maxine laughed easily. 'I was merely hoping that we could enjoy a friendly lunch together.' She paused expectantly, but when Tricia remained silent, she said persuasively, 'Please ... will you come?'

Curiosity overruled Tricia's good sense, and she heard herself asking calmly, 'Where shall I meet you?'

Maxine mentioned a small restaurant in town which Tricia knew well. 'Shall I expect you there soon after one o'clock, then?'

Tricia replied in the affirmative, but before she could ring off, Maxine added hastily, 'Don't tell Kyle, will you?'

The line went dead, and Tricia stared at the receiver in her hand with a curious expression in her eyes. Why should Kyle not be told about her meeting Maxine in town for lunch? Would he object if he knew, or was there, after all, an ulterior motive behind this supposedly friendly invitation from Maxine? she wondered nervously as she replaced the receiver on its cradle. It was possible that Kyle might have forbidden Maxine to have anything to do with her, in which case it would be typical of Maxine to go against his wishes. To forbid Maxine something had always encouraged her to behave obstinately in the past, and Tricia could not help wondering if this could be one of those occasions when Maxine's obstinacy was making her act against Kyle's wishes.

She thrust aside her thoughts when the post was brought in to her and, glancing ruefully at her cold cup of tea, she scanned through the letters and sorted them into an order of importance before taking them through to Kyle.

*

It was a few minutes after one when Tricia arrived at the restaurant, and after a quick glance across the already crowded interior, she warily made her way towards the corner table where Maxine awaited her. Dressed in a chic beige suit with an emerald green scarf adding a dash of colour, Maxine succeeded in making Tricia feel dowdy in her plain tweed skirt and matching jacket, but she was temporarily so engrossed in Maxine's sophistication and beauty, that she was oblivious of the admiring glances directed at herself.

Maxine smiled at Tricia when they faced each other across the checkered tablecloth. The smile, however, went no further than her crimson lips, and as Tricia looked into those cold green eyes she knew that Maxine was still very much the same vindictive person she had always been, but Tricia sensed somehow that she was now infinitely more dangerous.

'It's nice to see you again, Tricia.'

'Is it?' Tricia queried guardedly.

'You've changed quite a bit, though, but perhaps it's your new hair-style,' Maxine remarked, pouting her lips in the old, faintly sulky manner as she observed Tricia intently. 'I wish I could cut my hair, but in my profession long hair is usually an asset.'

'Are you on holiday?' Tricia asked with polite interest.

'Oh, goodness, no!' Maxine exclaimed, gesturing dramatically with her slender, manicured hands. 'I had to see Kyle about something important, so I took two days off from work. I'm leaving again this afternoon.'

The waiter arrived to take their order, and while

they waited they discussed the weather, the newly erected tourist attractions in Knysna, and several other impersonal subjects, but to Tricia it felt as though they were circling each other mentally like two wary jungle cats, assessing each other's strength, searching for possible weak points, and then deciding on the best tactical behaviour.

Tricia heaved an inward sigh of relief when their lunch was served, but she found she was too tense to enjoy the exquisitely prepared salad, and she did little more than shovel her food about her plate until their coffee was served. They eyed each other warily once more, and then it was Maxine who launched the attack.

'I must say I was surprised to learn that you never left Knysna.'

Taken aback, despite the fact that she had prepared herself mentally for this, Tricia asked carefully, 'Was there any reason why I should have left?'

'Well, I thought—considering everything that happened——' Maxine paused, lifted her shoulders in a slightly careless gesture, and smiled coldly. 'You know what I mean.'

Tricia stiffened. 'As far as I can recall, I had no cause to run away, Maxine. You made very sure that Kyle would never believe me even if I did decide to reveal the truth. You knew at the time that he was suspicious of me, that he considered me a fortune-hunter, and you also knew that, despite everything, he would take your word against mine without hesitation because he adored you and believed in you.' She drew a deep breath to steady herself before continuing. 'Unlike Benjamin, Kyle has always been blind to your faults, so what chance did I have to defend myself then, and what chance do I have to do so now?'

'That's true, I suppose,' Maxine admitted thoughtfully. 'It would have been your word against mine, and I knew Kyle would believe me, just as he would believe me now. Do remember that, won't you?'

'You've made your point, but I'm beginning to wonder why my silence is of such importance to you.'

Maxine smiled that cold, hard smile. 'I don't want Kyle to be hurt any more than he's been hurt already.'

Derisive laughter rose in Tricia's throat, but she caught it back sharply and managed to ask rather weakly, 'Hurt by whom?'

'By you, and women like yourself who want only his money,' Maxine replied without hesitation, and with astonishing audacity.

'You're the only one who could hurt Kyle, and you're wrong about one thing, Maxine,' Tricia told her coldly. 'I don't need Kyle's money.'

'You weren't squeamish about taking a large portion of Benjamin's, though,' Maxine remarked in a voice that was so sweet that it was venomous, but Tricia was not without ammunition of her own.

'If I remember correctly, Maxine, *you* were the one who was always in such a desperate need of money. Perhaps you still are,' she added coldly, realising that she had scored an unexpected hit when she saw the other girl flush deeply, but she was in no mood to continue the conversation, and as she rose to her feet she said: 'I'll pick up the tab for this most enlightening lunch.'

'Just a minute!' Maxine's fingernails bit into her wrist, and Tricia saw again that flicker of fear she had seen the evening before in those beautiful green eyes. 'Can I depend on your silence?'

Tricia disengaged her hand from Maxine's grasp, and frowned down at the marks her nails had left on her skin as she said bitterly, 'I've kept silent for six years, Maxine. Another thirty-six years wouldn't make any difference, and by that time we would all be too old to care.'

Maxine regained her confidence with remarkable swiftness, and she smiled again that mirthless smile that never quite reached her eyes. 'You're very wise.'

'Goodbye, Maxine!' Tricia bit out the words, unable to keep the note of disgust out of her voice. 'I hope we never have to see each other again.'

Tricia's head was throbbing when she reached the office, and she was in no mood to be harassed by Kyle, she decided fiercely when he cocked a quizzical eyebrow at her for swallowing down the second lot of aspirins that day, but, surprisingly, he said nothing, and continued on his way through her office to enter his own.

She worked at a feverish pace that afternoon, ridding herself of her pent-up anger. The dreadful suspicion grew in her mind that Frank might have been right about Maxine wanting to marry Kyle. No matter how painful the idea was to her, she had to admit to herself that the possibility did exist that Maxine might have wanted to make certain of her silence to ensure that her plans to marry Kyle were not spoiled.

Tricia tried not to think about it, telling herself that it was none of her business, and it was only with the greatest effort that she finally succeeded.

It was almost time to go home when Tricia returned a file to Kyle's office and found him standing beside the desk studying the plans which the architect had delivered to him that afternoon.

'Come here a minute,' he said without looking up and, as she crossed the room to stand beside him, he gestured with a wave of his hand towards the architectural drawings spread out before him. 'What do you think of the plans for the new offices and mill?'

Tricia stared down at the plans with a mixture of sadness and rebellion in her heart. The old familiar buildings would make way for modern structures of concrete and steel, and so a part of Knysna's historical background would be wiped out completely.

'It looks very impressive,' she said at last. 'And very much in keeping with the prestige of Union Timber.'

'What are you getting at this time?' Kyle demanded harshly.

'Nothing,' she snapped, pointing to something on the plans and changing the subject. 'What's that?'

'That's going to be the new furniture factory, and it will be equipped with the most modern and advanced machinery to cope with the demand,' he explained with surprising amiability.

'If you're going into the furniture business on such a large scale, then you'll need a showroom,' she remarked, wishing he would give her permission to leave so that she could escape from his disturbing presence.

'That's a good idea,' he said slowly, his eyes flicking over her with interest. 'A very good idea.'

'Glad you think so.'

His eyes held hers for several breathless seconds before she looked away, avoiding his probing glance for fear of what he might see, and knowing the extent of her own vulnerability at that moment.

'Have dinner with me at my hotel this evening?' he invited, and his voice was all at once like a warm caress, persuasive and exciting, but somehow she succeeded in resisting the temptation.

'No,' she refused him in a brittle voice, and then, almost as an afterthought, she added. 'Thank you.'

A faint smile curved his hard, chiselled mouth. 'You sound very definite.'

'I am,' she insisted, edging away from him nervously to place some distance between them.

'Why?'

'We agreed to stay out of each other's way, remember,' she reminded him bluntly, and after a brooding little silence Kyle nodded his head abruptly.

'So we did,' he acknowledged stonily as he turned away from her, and, dismissing herself, she left his office and closed the door firmly behind her.

She felt safer with a wall between them, but, until it was time for him to return to Cape Town, she would not feel entirely safe again.

CHAPTER SIX

THE peculiar feeling that she was being followed took possession of Tricia that evening when she drove home from work, but when she glanced in the rear-view mirror she saw only a large truck which took the turn-off eventually towards the main road. She chided herself for allowing her imagination to get the better of her, and concentrated instead on the traffic, but she could not rid herself entirely of that feeling. When she garaged her car some minutes later she looked about her nervously for a moment, almost as if she expected someone to jump out from nowhere to accost her, but nothing unusual happened to disturb the tranquillity of the neighbourhood.

Laughing at herself eventually for being so ridiculous, she entered the building through the back entrance, but her heart leapt into her throat when she saw Kyle's tall, muscular frame leaning against the wall in the foyer close to the lift.

'What are you doing here?' she demanded in a choked voice as he pushed himself away from the wall and came towards her.

'I've been waiting for you.'

She tilted her head back and stared up at him thoughtfully. 'Did you follow me here?'

'Yes,' he admitted unashamedly, thumbing the lift button.

Suspicion filled her eyes. 'Why? What do you want?'

'I want to talk to you.'

'You want to insult me, you mean,' she retorted hotly when she saw that cynical smile twisting his lips.

'Come on,' he said harshly as the lift doors slid open, but when she hung back, her arm was taken roughly and she was pushed inside unceremoniously. Kyle pressed the button for the fourth floor, and she shrank as far away from him as the confined space would allow when the lift came into motion.

'I have no intention of inviting you into my flat, so you're wasting your time.'

'In that case we'll have to talk here,' he announced harshly, the line of his jaw hard and unrelenting as he pressed the emergency stop button, causing the lift to come to an instant and shuddering halt between floors.

'Are you crazy,' she cried in alarm, making a dive for the control buttons, but his arm shot out in front of her, barring her way.

'Do I come up with you, or do we set the tongues wagging by spending the night here in the lift?'

Tricia fell back against the wall, helpless tears pricking her eyelids as the realisation swept through her that he was quite capable of carrying out his threat to hold her a prisoner in the lift, and, taking a steadying breath, she said grudgingly, 'Oh, very well! Come up, then, if you must!'

A gleam of triumph glittered in his eyes as he pressed the required button to set the lift in motion once more, but Tricia maintained a rigid silence until they entered her flat.

'Well?' she demanded irritably, taking off her coat and draping it over the back of a chair before she turned to face him. 'What did you want to talk to me about?'

'Offer me something to drink, and invite me to share your dinner with you. After that I might tell you.'

Incredulous anger sparkled in her dark eyes. 'You've got a nerve!'

'You certainly have a wonderful view of the lagoon from here,' he remarked with infuriating calmness, turning his back on her and walking towards the window. 'My hotel room unfortunately faces the other way.'

She stared at the formidable width of his back in frustration and anger for a moment, wishing she could do him a physical injury, then her lips tightened resignedly, and she marched into the kitchen to put on the kettle. It would be useless to try and reason with Kyle, for he could be as stubborn as a mule when it suited him. She could only hope that, after sharing her dinner with her, he would say what he had to say, and then get out.

When she took a cup of coffee through to him some minutes later, she found he had removed his jacket and tie and was relaxing quite comfortably in her favourite chair with a cigarette burning between his fingers. He looked tired, she thought with a sudden rush of unexpected tenderness, but when she became aware of those narrowed, watchful eyes resting on her, she hardened her heart and hurriedly placed his cup of coffee on the low table beside his chair before returning to the kitchen.

She worked quickly and deftly while she prepared a hasty meal of steak, fresh vegetables, and a salad. She had nothing else to offer him at such short notice, and, considering that he had had the audacity to invite himself, he would just have to take it or leave it, she decided irritably.

She was taking tomatoes and lettuce out of the refrigerator when she looked up to see Kyle strolling into the kitchen, and a flicker of alarm rippled through her. She turned away to rinse the tomatoes under the tap, but her insides shook nervously as she felt his eyes on her, observing her every movement.

'Could I help you with anything?' he asked at length when she had to leave the salad to see to the steak.

'No, thank you.'

'I'm quite good at making a salad,' he announced mockingly.

'Please, Kyle, this kitchen is much too small for two people,' she said stiffly, flinging him an angry glance over her shoulder, and, shrugging, he walked out again, leaving her in peace once more to see to the dinner she had been instructed to prepare for him.

Tricia was silent and edgy when they finally faced each other across the small stinkwood table. She felt his tawny glance resting on her from time to time while they ate, and nervousness finally made her push her half-empty plate aside to pour their coffee.

He smiled at her unexpectedly across the rim of his cup. 'The last time you cooked a meal for me was——'

'You don't have to remind me,' she interrupted him in a choked voice, her hand shaking to such an extent that she almost spilled some of her coffee into the saucer at the vivid recollection of that night in his yacht.

'We had tinned stew and mushrooms, and, if I'm

not mistaken, I made us an excellent cup of instant coffee afterwards.'

'Kyle——'

'There was a full moon that night,' he continued relentlessly, each word like the thrust of a sword, prodding her memory with painful precision. 'It shone into the cabin eventually when we put out the lights.'

Her cup clattered into her saucer, spilling some of the hot liquid on to her hand, but she was too upset to feel the sting. 'I don't want to talk about it,' she said coldly, dabbing absently at her hand with her table napkin.

'You may not want to talk about it, but you've never forgotten it, have you?' he insisted, his voice deepening with a degree of sensuality that quickened her pulse rate and made her body feel heated as he forced her, against her will, to remember something she would have given anything to forget. 'What happened that night was worth remembering. We——'

'Shut up!' she cried in anguish, almost knocking over her chair as she jumped to her feet. A film of perspiration had formed on her feverish brow, and she shook uncontrollably as she stood facing him across the table, her eyes darkened with pain, and her hands clenched so tightly at her sides that her nails bit agonisingly into her palms. 'Is this some new form of torture, Kyle?' she demanded hoarsely, her lips quivering so much that she could hardly control them. 'Haven't I suffered enough? Must I go on paying for something I—— Oh, Lord, what's the use?' she moaned, burying her face in her hands and turning away.

'Let's forget about the unpleasantness of the past.

Just for tonight let's remember instead those brief hours we shared together.' He was beside her now, his hands warm against her shoulders as he turned her to face him, and the look on his taut features conveyed his feelings even before he muttered thickly, 'I want you, Tricia.'

'No!' she cried huskily, recoiling from him mentally, but there was no escape from the hands that held her, and the burning intensity of those peculiar eyes that seemed to want to delve deep into the hidden recesses of her mind.

'You won't regret it.'

'Won't I?' she asked cynically, grasping at every available straw as she felt him sapping her resistance with his nearness. 'And what label will you find to attach to me this time? Harlot?'

'Tricia!'

'Why not?' she demanded, staring up into eyes that registered mild shock. 'That's what you made me feel like the other day when I wanted to apologise for my behaviour, and you offered me money for "kisses and a little light lovemaking" as you called it.'

His mouth tightened. 'That was regrettable.'

'Yes,' she agreed in a choked voice, straining away from him. 'And so were a good many other things I could think of.'

'Forget the past, damn you!' he groaned, dragging her against him with a force that temporarily robbed her of her breath, and the desire to resist. His one arm was like a steel band about her waist, foiling her eventual attempts to escape, while his free hand became entangled in the dark, silky hair at the nape of her neck, preventing her from further attempts to avoid his descending lips.

The fiery passion of his kiss was like a devouring flame, and her resistance tumbled like a house of cards to leave her trembling on the very brink of desire.

'I could have you now, if I wanted to, without encountering much resistance from you,' he murmured triumphantly against her lips while his fingers caressed the smoothness of her throat to linger persuasively where her pulse throbbed wildly in response to his touch.

'I know that,' she whispered breathlessly, but, as she felt his heartbeat quicken beneath her hands, she fought her way back to sanity through the mist of her desire, adding, 'And just think how we shall despise ourselves, *and* each other, tomorrow.'

'You can't deny that you want me, Tricia,' he stated with a touch of that hateful arrogance in his voice, and the spell he had cast over her was suddenly shattered.

She escaped the sweet prison of his arms before he had time to guess her intentions and, after hastily placing some distance between them, she said unsteadily, 'No, I don't deny it. To deny that I want you would be like denying myself the air that I breathe. It's humiliating for me to have to admit this, but despite the way I feel, I won't be used by you, Kyle. Not again.'

His eyebrows rose fractionally. 'Who said anything about using you?'

'Isn't that what this amounts to?' she demanded, resorting to anger as a defence against the tears which threatened to choke her. 'You want me to go to bed with you, but where exactly does that leave me?'

The change that occurred in Kyle's appearance

was almost frightening. His eyes became glacially cold, and the lean jaw grew taut with suppressed fury.

'I get it,' he said cynically, his shoulder muscles flexing beneath the expensive cotton of his shirt with the effort to control himself. 'You want marriage. Twenty thousand Rand out of my father's estate was not enough for you, and you've decided you want more. Marriage to me would naturally give you more, so you won't settle for anything less, will you?'

She was tempted to suggest that that assumption would be more correct if it were directed at Maxine and not at herself, but she decided against it, and if she had ever dwelt on the slender hope that Kyle might one day condescend to ask her to marry him, then that hope had now been brutally dashed. To him she was nothing more than an object of desire, and he could quite easily walk out of her life within the next few days and forget her existence just as he had done six years ago, but this time she would not allow him to leave her life in ruins as he had done once before.

'I don't want your money, Kyle,' she told him in a flat, emotionless voice, 'and I'm not suggesting that you marry me either. What I would like very much at this moment is for you to go away and leave me in peace.'

His mouth twisted derisively as he shrugged himself into his jacket and pushed his tie into the pocket, and his eyes raked her insolently from head to foot as he said contemptuously, 'You sound so virtuous, but I know that you're not, and that underneath that façade you're still the same scheming little bitch my father once picked up.'

'It's the other way round, Kyle,' she reminded him coldly, feeling as though something had died inside of her. '*I* picked your father up.'

'Literally and figuratively, yes,' he stormed at her. 'And you made damn sure that you got something for your trouble!'

The front door slammed behind him moments later, and she was still standing where he had left her, staring blankly at nothing in particular, when the doorbell rang, jolting her nerves sharply, and bringing her painfully back to life. It couldn't be Kyle returning to apologise, she thought cynically as she went to answer it, and she was relieved to discover that her assumption had been correct when she found Frank standing on her doorstep.

'Was that Kyle Hammond I passed on the way up?' he asked as she closed the door and led the way through to the lounge.

'It was.'

'I thought so.'

'He invited himself to dinner,' she heard herself explaining stiffly when she intercepted Frank's curious glance straying across the room. 'I'll clear the table quickly and make a fresh pot of coffee.'

Tricia washed the dishes and left them on the rack to dry while she waited for the kettle to boil, but she was only vaguely aware of what she was doing. Her life had become a nightmare from which there seemed to be no escape, and she was suddenly afraid—*desperately* afraid! The past was closing in on her like the tightening of a fisherman's net, bringing with it all the fear, heartache and despair she had once thought was behind her. She could not bear to go through another period like the one she had been through before, but now, after all those years, Kyle seemed determined to take his revenge, and, because of her love for him, he had it in his power to hurt her more than he could ever imagine.

'You never brought your car to the garage this afternoon for its regular service,' Frank remarked when she eventually brought the tray of coffee through to the lounge.

She glanced up with a start. 'I'm afraid I forgot all about it.'

'I'll take your car when I go home, and leave mine outside for you to use,' he said calmly. 'I should have your car serviced and back here by tomorrow evening.'

Tricia felt guilty that he should go to so much trouble for her, but she had discovered in the past that it was futile to object, so she merely smiled her thanks and poured their coffee.

Seated beside Frank's bulky figure on the small sofa, she observed him unobtrusively at first, and then with growing interest. Here was a way of escape from her nightmare existence, she thought distractedly, and, although she tried to discard the idea, it lingered until, against her will, she found that it began to appeal to her. Frank would be a kind and gentle husband, and he would never deliberately do anything to hurt her. With him she would feel safe and secure for the rest of her life, and he would be the shield she needed so desperately against any attack Kyle might wish to launch.

'It's selfish of you to want to use him,' her heart warned, but her mind argued, 'Why not? He loves you, and you care enough for him to be able to make such a marriage work.'

Heart and mind fought a fierce and silent battle, but when she thought of what Kyle could do to her again, she finally came to a decision which she hoped she would not live to regret.

'Frank ...' she began calmly, but her trembling hand betrayed her when she placed her empty cup in the tray. 'There've never been any secrets between us. We've known each other for six years, and you know just about everything there is to know about me.'

'That's true.'

She met his steady blue gaze for a moment, then lowered her eyes again nervously to her tightly clenched hands in her lap. 'Do—do you still want to—to marry me?'

'What kind of a question is that?' he laughed softly. 'Of course I still want to marry you. Haven't I asked you often enough over the past years to convince you of that?'

'I—well, I—if you still do, then I—I——'

'Are you trying to tell me you've changed your mind?' he queried gently when she began to falter doubtfully.

Tricia hesitated, her knuckles whitening as she laced her fingers together tightly, and then she nodded abruptly. 'Yes,' she whispered, 'I've changed my mind.'

There! She had said it! She had committed herself, and quite suddenly she wanted to burst into tears.

'Tricia ...' He placed a gentle but firm hand beneath her chin and raised her face to his, but he shook his head slowly when his tender, searching glance took in her quivering lips, and the haunted expression in her dark eyes. 'No,' he assured her softly, 'I'm not going to ask unnecessary, awkward questions. I'm just going to be grateful for whatever it was that made you change your mind and finally agree to marry me.'

Tears welled up in her eyes and tightened her throat. 'Frank, I——'

'I know,' he interrupted gently, his fingers tracing the delicate curve of her cheek. 'You don't love me, but I love you enough for both of us, and I swear I'll spend the rest of my life trying to make you happy.'

Tenderness and love shone out of his eyes, but they were the wrong eyes, her heart mourned, and all at once she could no longer keep the hot, scalding tears in check as they spilled over on to her pale cheeks.

'I don't deserve that you should love me,' she sobbed against his shoulder, but his arms went about her instantly, and she was cradled against him very much like a small child in need of comfort.

'Hush, my dear,' he whispered softly just above her ear while he stroked her dark curls and allowed her to cry until she felt curiously drained.

He held her without kissing her, and for quite some time that seemed to be enough for him, but when he finally found her lips with his own, she kissed him back with a wealth of feeling that stemmed from her desperate need to shut out the tantalising memory of those other arms and lips which were forbidden to her.

When Frank eventually went home, she took a

leisurely, relaxing bath and went to bed. She felt exhausted, but found that she could not sleep, and after tossing about restlessly for more than an hour she got up and swallowed down a tablet as she had been forced to do the night before.

The shrill, persistent ringing of the telephone woke her some hours later and, dragging herself out of bed, she went through to the lounge to answer it while she silently cursed whoever it was for dialling the wrong number at that hour of the night.

'Were you asleep?' Kyle's deep, familiar voice wanted to know.

'What do you think?' she demanded indignantly, lowering herself on to the arm of a nearby chair.

'Alone?'

The word was shot at her, but despite her drugged state of mind she realised that he was referring to Frank, and his deliberate insinuation, that Frank had remained the night to share her bed, made her blood boil.

'Go to hell!' she croaked angrily, slamming the receiver back on to its cradle, and telling herself she did not really care what he thought.

Fuming inwardly, she stumbled back to bed and switched off the light, and, despite her fears, her head barely touched the pillow before she was asleep once more, giving her no time to ponder over Kyle's hateful telephone call.

Something disturbed her again, however, and she stirred restlessly in her sleep, dragging the blankets with her when she rolled over on to her other side, but the persistent ringing of a bell finally penetrated the mistiness of her deep slumber. She fumbled about in the darkness to silence the alarm, but she sat up in bed with a jerk when the alarm button refused to budge, realising now that the sound which had awakened her was that of someone leaning heavily on her doorbell. For a moment she could not move as she hovered between terror and the overpowering desire to drift back into sleep, but she pulled herself together and switched on the bedside lamp to squint at the time. *Two o'clock!*

'Who on earth can it be?' she muttered aloud, reaching for her gown and pushing her feet into her soft mules.

The ringing continued relentlessly as she staggered through the lounge, switching on lights as she made her way to the door, but the doorbell stopped ringing the moment she flicked the switch for the hall light, and the deathly silence that followed seemed almost eerie.

'Who is it?' she demanded unsteadily through the door.

'Kyle.'

She expelled the air from her lungs as fear made way for incredulous surprise, but then a slow anger began to churn inside of her as she snapped, 'Go away!'

'Open this door, or I'll wake the entire building,' he threatened, and, deciding against the embarrassment of having to explain the incident to her neighbours, she unhooked the safety chain and turned the key in the lock.

'Kyle, are you mad?' she demanded in a hoarse whisper as he pushed past her unceremoniously.

'I'm beginning to suspect so,' he growled throatily, walking towards the lounge with purposeful strides.

Tricia closed the door and followed him a little dazedly, her drugged mind momentarily unable to grasp the reason for his visit at this late hour, and why he should find it necessary to storm into her bedroom only to emerge again a few moments later. He had changed into beige slacks and a green, turtle-necked sweater since leaving her earlier that evening she noticed distractedly as he came towards her, and his eyes looked oddly wild when they met hers.

'May I know what you hoped to find in my bedroom?' she wanted to know, blinking up at him a little stupidly.

'Frank Carlson,' he shot the words at her. 'Where have you hidden him?'

Her body still felt lethargic, but her mind was now crystal clear as she began to understand the reason for Kyle's behaviour.

'I haven't hidden him anywhere,' she said coldly. 'He went home hours ago.'

'What's his car doing outside, then?'

'He took my car in to his garage for a service, and left me his to get to work with in the morning,' she explained angrily. 'What's it to you, anyway?'

His eyes narrowed, but his threatening attitude seemed to diminish. 'I was curious.'

'Curious? At two in the morning?' she demanded incredulously, then she moaned softly and swayed towards a chair, gripping the back of it so tightly that her fingers ached. 'For heaven's sake, Kyle, go away and leave me in peace!'

Kyle was beside her in a flash, a strong, steadying arm about her sagging shoulders. 'What's wrong with you?' he demanded.

'It's nothing,' she muttered, trying to shake off the disturbing intimacy of his touch, and wishing the room would stop swivelling about her. 'I took a sleeping tablet before I went to bed, and I'm practically asleep on my feet, that's all.'

'What kind of tablet?' he demanded abruptly. 'Show me.'

'Let me go!' she cried, twisting herself free of his arm and stumbling away from him, but his fingers snaked about her wrist to apply a merciless pressure.

'Show me!'

'You're hurting me,' she gasped, blinking away the tears that filled her eyes, and shrinking physically from his menacing expression as he towered over her.

'I'll hurt you more if you don't let me have a look at those tablets.'

'If you must know, they're in the middle drawer of my dressing table,' she said at last, and found herself practically jerked off her feet as he dragged her after him into her bedroom.

With the phial of tablets lying in the palm of his hand, he released her, and stared down at the label with his brows drawn together in a deep frown. 'How many did you take?'

'One as prescribed,' she replied tiredly, nursing her wrist.

'Are you sure?'

'Oh, for God's sake, Kyle! Why this sudden concern for my welfare?' she demanded, her temper flaring.

He returned the phial of tablets to the drawer and closed it carefully before he turned to face her, his expression inscrutable. 'I'm damned if I know why I worry about you, because you certainly don't deserve my concern.'

The light of the bedside lamp played over his taut, angry face, accentuating the fairness of his hair, and the square, jutting jaw beneath that faintly sensuous mouth. Tiredness overwhelmed her suddenly, and she sat down heavily on the bed when her legs began to shake uncontrollably beneath her.

'Please, Kyle,' she sighed, brushing her hair out of her eyes with a trembling hand. 'It's two o'clock in the morning. 'You've satisfied yourself that I'm alone, and that I haven't taken an overdose of tablets, now would you mind going.'

'How often do you take these tablets?' he persisted infuriatingly with his questioning.

'Not often. This is only the second time in some years, but ...' She looked up suddenly, her eyes sparkling with renewed anger. 'What are you doing up at this ungodly hour, anyway?'

'I couldn't sleep, so I went for a drive.'

His penetrating glance flicked over her, and all at once his presence in her bedroom suggested a certain intimacy that sent a rosy flush up into her pale cheeks. She was aware now of her touselled hair, and her face devoid of make-up, but most of all she was conscious of the flimsiness of her night attire as she pulled her gown closer about her and tightened the belt.

The silence between them was becoming charged with emotion and, sensing danger in every quivering nerve of her body, she said huskily, 'Please go back to your hotel, Kyle.'

He stood motionless, but she knew somehow that

every muscle in his tall, lean body was geared for action, and her treacherous pulse quickened with nervous excitement when he said thickly, 'Let me stay.'

There was temptation in the very stillness of him, but, knowing how vulnerable she would be at that moment if he should resort to physical persuasion, she came to a quick decision.

'I can't let you stay,' she heard herself say in a voice unlike her own. 'I shall be handing in my resignation tomorrow, and I'm going to marry Frank as soon as he can arrange it.'

Did she imagine it, or did she see Kyle flinch? she wondered distractedly, but there was no mistaking the peculiar whiteness which had settled about his mouth as he exclaimed harshly, 'You can't marry him!'

'You're not in a position to dictate to me, Kyle,' she reminded him coldly. 'I can and I *will* marry Frank, and I don't need your permission to do so.'

She saw his hands clench into fists at his sides, and a shiver raced through her, making her feel as though she had signed her own death warrant by telling him of her decision. She kept her head lowered, afraid to meet his eyes, but the next instant she saw him turn on his heel and stride out of her room. She heard the front door close behind him, and a few moments later she staggered through the lounge into the hall. There was a mist before her eyes making her fumble with the chain and key, but it was only when she passed a shaky hand across her tired eyes that she realised she was crying, and, no matter how much she tried to control herself, the tears continued to flow strongly.

She somehow managed to get back into bed, and, hardly aware of what she was doing, she murmured Kyle's name over and over despairingly while her fingers clutched at the silver falcon about her neck as if it were a lifeline.

'If only you'd trusted me and believed in me a little,' she sobbed into her damp pillow, and then, mercifully, she was asleep, and this time she slept undisturbed until the early morning sunshine stole in through her window.

David McGregor arrived from the Cape Town offices of Union Timber that morning to take over the management of Barrett's. He was young, with alert grey eyes, and plenty of drive, and his smiling presence in the office eased a great deal of the tension between Tricia and Kyle during the remainder of that week.

Tricia knew that Kyle would be leaving Knysna shortly, and the realisation brought with it a certain amount of relief, as well as a great deal of pain. Her neatly typed resignation lay on his desk, and in four weeks she, too, would be leaving Barrett's, to marry Frank. It was unlikely that she would ever see Kyle again, and perhaps that was as it should be if she hoped to make a success of her marriage.

She intended to have an early night on the Thursday evening, but Frank arrived at her flat shortly after seven, and he looked oddly like a small boy who had been at the forbidden biscuit tin. He took her into his arms and kissed her with unaccustomed passion before he slipped a ring on to her finger, and she was speechless for a moment as she stared down at the sparkling cluster of diamonds set in gold.

There was an ache deep down inside her that would never be assuaged entirely. The longing for Kyle would always be there, but with luck, and plenty of determination, she was positive she could find a certain measure of happiness with this man who had stood by her so loyally in the past.

She looked up into Frank's anxious grey eyes, and forced a smile to her lips. 'It's beautiful.'

His features relaxed and, slipping her arms about his neck, she raised her lips to his, inviting his kiss almost desperately in an effort to wipe Kyle's image from her mind.

'Get your coat, we're going out to celebrate,' he announced eventually, and a few minutes later they were driving out to a small restaurant just out of town.

Over shrimps and champagne they toasted each other, and as she observed his delighted, faintly boyish expression, she felt convinced that she had, after all, made the right decision. It was futile crying for something she could not have, and it would be far more sensible to try to make something of what she already had. Frank would take care of her, she had no doubt of that, and she would eventually find solace in his love for her.

CHAPTER SEVEN

IT was late on Friday afternoon when Tricia found herself alone with Kyle for the first time since that night he had come to her flat. David McGregor had gone down to the mill to check up on a delayed order, and Kyle was preparing for his meeting with an important new client from up country. They spoke to each other in monosyllables as they checked through the papers he required, avoiding each other's eyes, and upholding the barrier between them. Once or twice she noticed his tawny glance resting on the ring sparkling on her finger and, except for a slight tightening of his lips, his expression remained inscrutable, giving her no indication of his feelings.

She was searching for a file which Kyle required when the door opened unexpectedly and Maxine burst into the office. Slim and elegant in a leather coat and knee-high boots, she advanced purposefully towards the desk, and a quick glance at Kyle's face told Tricia that he was equally as surprised to see his stepsister. Instead of a welcoming smile, however, his mouth tightened ominously, and a frown settled between his heavy brows.

'I thought I told you not to come here again.'

'I wanted to talk to you, Kyle,' she replied, flicking her green glance meaningfully at Tricia who stood clutching the file to her breast as if it were a shield. 'Privately,' Maxine added in clear, decisive tones.

'Stay where you are!' Kyle snapped as Tricia turned towards the door, and she obeyed meekly, aware of an unusual tension hovering in the air when he transferred his attention back to Maxine. 'You had no right to come in here unannounced, and whatever it is you want to talk about will have to wait. I happen to be extremely busy, and in a few minutes I have to go out.'

Maxine threw back her head in a familiar gesture of angry defiance that struck an unpleasant chord in Tricia's memory. 'I've waited long enough for you to make up your mind one way or the other!'

'Get out, Maxine, and let me get on with my work,' he ordered sharply, ignoring her as he continued to inspect the contents of his briefcase.

Maxine's eyes glittered with unmistakable fury, and Tricia cringed inwardly as she fought against the nightmare sensation that she was being swept back in time to that warm summer afternoon when she had witnessed that furious and fatal argument between Benjamin Hammond and his step-daughter. This time, however, the argument was between Kyle and Maxine, but the atmosphere was equally electrifying.

'Damn you, Kyle!' Maxine finally exploded, blind now to Tricia's presence in the room. 'I want that money, and I mean to have it.'

'No way, Maxine,' Kyle countered disdainfully. 'Neither you nor that sexy friend of yours know anything about managing a business. I suggest you both stick to posing for the cameras, or parading up and down ramps for the benefit of the buying public, and forget about wasting your money on something as precarious as this beauty salon.'

'We wouldn't be wasting our money. The salon is flourishing at the moment, and you're just being pig-headed about——'

'The salon you're referring to has never flourished as a business, and never will,' Kyle interrupted her in a thundering voice that made Tricia, as an onlooker, flinch nervously. 'The owners are up to their eyeballs in debt, and I'm not allowing you to throw away good money on a worthless project.'

'It's *my* money, Kyle, and I'll do with it as I damn well please!' Maxine shouted, her beautiful face distorted with rage.

'You damn well won't! Not while I have any say in the matter,' Kyle returned coldly, controlling himself with an obvious effort. 'It's time I left for that appointment. Give me that file, Tricia ... and what the devil have I done with my car keys?' he added irritably.

'I have them,' Maxine announced coolly, pouncing on the small bunch of keys before Kyle or Tricia were able to do anything about it and, dangling them between forefinger and thumb, she opened up her coat and dropped them down the front of her sweater. There was now a gleam of triumph in her eyes as she faced Kyle. 'You may have them back the moment you've written out a cheque for the required amount, so be sensible, darling.'

Tricia shrank back against the filing cabinet and held her breath. The nightmare was now complete. The action had been replayed, but on this occasion the opposition was not a frail old man gasping for breath, and Tricia glanced fearfully from one to the other in the deathly silence which reigned. Maxine had the appearance of someone supremely confident of her victory; those tactics had worked so often before, and there was no reason why they should not work again now, but Kyle had gone strangely pale as he stared fixedly at Maxine.

'Is that what you did to Father?'

Those words from Kyle had been quietly, almost absently spoken, but they seemed to explode in Tricia's mind, shaking the foundations beneath her, and making her shrink further against the cold, hard cabinet behind her when she saw Maxine go a sickly shade of grey.

'How do you——?' Maxine began confusedly, biting back the remainder of her sentence, but it was too late, and she knew it. Those three words, spoken in an unguarded moment, had revealed the truth as clearly as if they had been painted in bold black letters against the white wall behind her, and the realisation seemed to unleash the fury of a wild-cat in her; a fury that was suddenly directed at Tricia who stood pale and motionless as Maxine lunged crazily at her and screamed, 'So you told him after all, you bitch!'

'*Hold it!*' Kyle had moved with incredible speed to grip Maxine's wrists a fraction of a second before those long, polished nails could tear at Tricia's un-protected face. Maxine tried to fight him off like someone demented, but Kyle was stronger, and he shook her mercilessly until the violence gradually ebbed from her. Defeated, she seemed to wilt like a parched flower, and Tricia felt a twinge of pity for her when Kyle eventually thrust her away from him with an exclamation of disgust. 'Tricia never told me anything, Maxine. It was you who gave yourself away. I should have guessed the truth long ago, but my stubborn belief that you could never stoop so low prevented me from doing so.'

Maxine recovered her composure with remarkable swiftness. 'I don't know what you're talking about.'

'Don't try to play dumb with me, Maxine,' Kyle said in harsh, clipped tones. 'I'm past the stage of being fooled by your "little girl innocent" act.'

During the chilling silence that followed his remark, Tricia was conscious of the heavy, painful beat of her heart as she stared anxiously at Kyle. Stripped of his illusions, he seemed to have aged considerably, and suddenly Tricia could not bear to see him look like that. 'I think I'll go through to my office.'

'Stay where you are!' Kyle ordered sharply, and Tricia froze beneath his stabbing glance. 'It was *you*, wasn't it, Maxine?' he continued in a deadly calm voice that sent shivers of fear up Tricia's spine as he focussed his attention on the younger girl once more. 'It was *you* who wanted money, and it was *you* who snatched away Father's tablets when he felt an attack coming on. Tricia managed to get the tablets away from you, but it was already too late, wasn't it, and that was when I walked into his room.' His eyes became glazed, and pain flashed across his features, leaving his square jaw taut. 'Oh, my God, I can see it all now. You accusing Tricia to save your own skin, and Tricia standing with the phial of tablets in her hand. The evidence was utterly damning, and I believed you, Maxine. Like a fool I believed you!'

Stripped of every vestige of the pretence which she had cultivated so carefully over the years, and knowing that she faced utter defeat, Maxine allowed both Kyle and Tricia to see her as she really was; a cold, ruthless, and calculating woman who would stop at nothing to achieve her ultimate goal.

'Since you seem to know so much already, you might as well know everything,' Maxine smiled twistedly, a mixture of defiance and resignation mirrored in those glittering, emerald-coloured eyes as they shifted from Kyle to Tricia and back. 'I'd always hoped you would one day ask me to marry you, Kyle. When Tricia first appeared on the scene you were suspicious of her, and I knew you disliked her as much as I did, so I never considered her a threat, but I began to hate her when I realised you were becoming more than generally interested in her. I never for a moment expected that anything serious would happen to Father that day, but when he died I seized at the opportunity to discredit her in your eyes. And I enjoyed doing it.'

'Get out of here, Maxine!' Kyle ordered in a voice that sounded hoarse and unfamiliar, and only then did Tricia risk opening her eyes, but she kept her glance rigidly averted from his.

'Certainly,' Maxine smiled coldly, but at the door she halted and, slipping her hand into the front of her sweater, she said: 'I almost forgot—here are your keys. They're no longer of any use to me.'

The keys fell on the carpet at Tricia's feet where Maxine had flung them, but neither she nor Kyle stooped to retrieve them as Maxine's footsteps echoed through the outer office. The door slammed behind her, rattling the windows in their wooden frames, and then Tricia could no longer avoid Kyle's searching, probing eyes.

Relying heavily on the remnants of her dignity,

she raised her glance to his, and what she saw shook her considerably. His pupils had become dilated to the extent that his eyes had the appearance of two black pools in his white, incredibly drawn face. He seemed to sway on his feet before her, and she reached out instinctively to steady him, but he was in control of himself before she could touch him, seemingly unaware of her concerned gesture as he continued to stare at her for endless seconds like someone in a stupor.

The ringing of the telephone mercifully broke the tense silence between them, and Tricia went through to her office to answer it, but retraced her steps a few seconds later to find that Kyle was still standing exactly where she had left him.

'I have Mr Bergman's secretary on the line. Mr Bergman wants to know if you're still coming to see him this afternoon?'

'Tell Mr Bergman's secretary——' he began aggressively, but then a look of angry resignation crossed his face. 'Tell Mr Bergman's secretary I'll be there in ten minutes.'

Tricia returned to her office to pass on the message, but when she replaced the receiver she turned to find Kyle standing beside her with his briefcase in his hand.

'I won't be returning to the office this afternoon, but we have to talk,' he said crisply, outwardly in control of himself, except for the dullness of his tawny eyes, and the taut line of his jaw which told her differently.

'There's nothing to talk about,' she hedged desperately, moving away from him until she had placed the width of her desk between them.

'I'll see you this evening at your flat.'

'No, I——'

'This evening,' he insisted adamantly, and a few moments later the outer door closed behind his departing figure.

Tricia sat down on the swivel chair behind her desk and buried her face in her hands. Her temples were throbbing painfully, but when she felt hysteria bubbling up inside her like a kettle on the boil, she left the office and hurried down the short passage towards the cloakroom. Once inside, she leaned against the door and closed her eyes, trying desperately to control herself, but she could not check the choking laughter that began to rack her slim body, and neither could she prevent the hot tears from coursing down her cheeks. Her head felt as if it wanted to burst when she finally succeeded in curbing her hysteria, and then, to her horror, she found herself fighting against the waves of nausea which threatened to overwhelm her. She knelt beside the basin, too exhausted to get to her feet when the nausea finally subsided, and then she wept again.

She had no idea how long she remained there, but her tears had dried on her cheeks when she eventually managed to get to her feet. She washed her hands and splashed cold water on to her face before she returned to her office, and was relieved to find that David McGregor had not yet returned from the mill. Her face looked ghastly in the small round mirror of her powder compact, but she hastily repaired the damage caused by the ravaging tears and added a touch of colour to her pale lips. David McGregor walked into the office moments after she had slipped her powder compact into her handbag, but she kept her face averted as he walked past her desk. To her dismay, he paused at the door to the inner office, and turned.

'Miss Meredith?' She had to look up then. 'Is there something the matter? Are you ill, perhaps?'

'No, I'm—I'm fine,' she lied, touched by his concern, but wishing he would go away and leave her in peace instead of hovering in the doorway and glancing at her in such a perturbed fashion.

'A headache?' he proffered sympathetically, and she grasped at his explanation, partly because it was true, and partly because it would explain the reason for her red-rimmed eyes without inviting further questions.

'Yes, I do happen to have a headache,' she said hastily.

'It's been rather tough on you these past few days with the chief breathing fire at us, and with me plying you with questions in order to find my way around.' His smile was warm and friendly, then he glanced up at the clock against the wall and said: 'Look, there's a half hour to go before closing time, and there's nothing to do at the moment except answer the telephone. Why don't you go home and relax? You have the weekend ahead of you, so take a tablet, and forget about everything.'

Forget about everything. Tricia almost laughed out loud, but, with her recent bout of hysteria still fresh in her memory, she pulled herself together sharply.

'I don't think Mr Hammond——'

'Mr Hammond won't know,' he cut in on her refusal. 'Get your coat on and go home.'

She hesitated only a moment, then she shelved her uncertainty and put on her coat as he had suggested. When she turned, he was still watching her.

'Thank you, Mr McGregor.'

'The name's David,' he corrected with a flashing smile. 'Enjoy your weekend.'

There was nothing enjoyable at the prospect of the weekend ahead of her; not with Kyle coming to see her that evening in order to rake over the past until every detail was uncovered, she thought dismally as she took the lift down to the ground floor.

When she arrived home she swallowed down a couple of tablets for her headache, and took a leisurely bath to ease the tension out of her weary body. She made herself something to eat, but the food seemed to lodge somewhere between her throat and her stomach, and she finally settled for a cup of black coffee with plenty of sugar. She turned on the radio and tried to relax, but the wild disco beat emanating from it exploded in her ears, and she leaned forward again to turn the radio off. She drank her coffee and tried not to think, but her mind continued to churn over the events which had taken place in the office that afternoon until her thoughts became frighteningly disjointed. The wheel of time had turned full circle, and it was ironic that it should have been Maxine herself who had inadvertently allowed the truth to come out. Maxine's actions had provoked Kyle into setting a trap for her, and she had walked into it quite unsuspectingly.

Tricia tried not to dwell on the subject, and went through to the kitchen to pour herself another cup of coffee, but she could not wipe Kyle's image from her mind. After learning the truth, he had stood swaying before her, his pallor a deathly white, stripped of his illusions as well as the cloak of arrogance which had always been such a vital part of him.

She lowered herself tiredly into her favourite chair and sipped her black, sweetened coffee. Through the window she watched the setting sun cast a crimson hue in the night sky where the seagulls circled lazily for the last time before nightfall, but the beauty of the scene escaped her at that moment as she thought of the confrontation that lay ahead of her. She stared down at the ring which she twisted absently about her finger, and wished that she could have asked Frank to be there with her when Kyle arrived, but she knew that what had to be said between Kyle and herself would be better said in private.

She shivered involuntarily when the room grew dark, but she did not switch on the lights. She found a certain tranquillity in the darkness that seemed to enfold her and ease the tension within her and, placing her empty cup on the low table before her, she leaned back in her chair with her eyes closed.

She started violently a few minutes later when the doorbell rang shrilly, and although she looked outwardly composed, her heart was beating heavily when she rose from her chair. That would be Kyle, and heaven only knew what lay in store for her, she thought with a certain amount of resignation as she switched on the lights and walked into the small entrance hall to let him in.

Kyle looked frighteningly grim when he followed Tricia into the lounge. He had loosened his tie carelessly, and his silvery hair looked as though his fingers had ploughed through it agitatedly at regular intervals. His chiselled mouth was drawn into a thin, hard line, and the muscles stood out sharply along the side of his lean jaw, giving the impression that his teeth were tightly clenched.

She gestured silently towards a chair, but he declined the invitation to sit down with a shake of his head, and paced the floor instead with his hands thrust deep into the pockets of his pants. His restlessness somehow transferred itself to her, and she remained standing, clasping and unclasping her hands behind her back like a child while she waited nervously for him to speak. He paused beside the window, standing with his back to her while he presumably stared down into the darkened street below, and out across the lagoon, then he turned and captured her wary glance with his dangerously compelling gaze.

'Why didn't you tell me, Tricia?' he demanded, lessening the distance between them with quick strides, and she shrank from him as well as the hint of savagery in his voice. 'Why didn't you defend yourself that day my father died instead of allowing me to believe all these years that you'd caused his death?'

'Would you have believed me had I denied Maxine's accusation?' she asked, unable to prevent a hint of sarcasm from creeping into her voice.

His eyes narrowed. 'After what had happened between us the day before you should have had more confidence in me.'

'After what had happened between us you shouldn't have been so willing to believe Maxine without suggesting that I was given a hearing.'

'Perhaps not,' he admitted roughly, 'but if you'd denied her accusation it would at least have raised a question of doubt in my mind.'

'That shouldn't have been necessary, but you were so prejudiced against me that you willingly grasped at anything and everything which would prove that I was exactly the sort of girl you thought me.'

'Damn you, Tricia, I had to protect my father's interests,' he exploded angrily, so close to her now that her senses stirred involuntarily at his nearness as she found herself staring up into his blazing eyes. 'I'd lost count of the women who'd walked in and out of my father's life since my stepmother's death, and they all had only one object in mind—*money*.' His heated glance swept over her, then he turned away and pushed his fingers agitatedly through his hair. 'What reason was there for me to suppose you were different from all the others? You were a woman, and no woman was above suspicion.'

There was bitterness in the smile that curved her lips. 'That supposition didn't include Maxine, naturally.'

'Maxine was my stepsister,' he explained harshly without turning. 'I'd noticed her grow from childhood, through adolescence to womanhood, and suspecting one's own family of lecherous behaviour is, or *was*, unthinkable. You would have felt the same had our positions been reversed.'

He turned then and faced her with a hint of the old arrogance in the glitter of his eyes, and in the carriage of his proud head. Tricia studied him briefly with a quick ache in her throat before she lowered her lashes to veil the emotions which began to stir in the depths of her soul.

'We're arguing round in circles,' she sighed exasperatedly. 'You and I were together the night before your father died. So what? I know now that I wasn't the first, and I don't suppose I was the last. I trusted you and believed in you that night, but when I saw how readily you accepted Maxine's version of what had occurred, I knew that deep down your opinion of me hadn't changed at all.'

'So you remained silent, and took the blame for something which you knew would make me hate and despise you for the rest of my life unless I discovered the truth elsewhere.'

'Yes.' She looked up then, and her eyes filled with helpless tears, but she blinked them away hastily. 'You had something that was very precious; something I would have given anything to possess. You had a family, and how could I break up something which I wanted so desperately for myself? You'd always doted on Maxine. You trusted her, and believed in her, and I knew I couldn't——'

'Go on,' he prompted quietly and insistently when she came to an abrupt halt, and his eyes followed the path of her trembling hand as she lifted it to her throat to ease away the ache.

'Your father was never blind to Maxine's faults, Kyle, but he never had the heart to disillusion you,' she managed at last, but the huskiness in her voice was more pronounced because of the tight control she exercised on it. 'What right had I to do what your father could never manage to do himself?'

She withstood his penetrating glance, praying that he would not question her further until she was forced to admit that she had initially taken the blame to protect him from the hurt he had eventually suffered at Maxine's own hands that afternoon, and that she had done so willingly, and because of her deep love for him; a love that must now remain hidden for ever.

He lit a cigarette and smoked it in silence while he paced the floor once more and, lowering herself on to the padded arm of the chair beside her, Tricia watched him anxiously, wondering at his thoughts, and more than just a little afraid of what still had to come. Several tension-packed seconds passed before he ceased his restless pacing and crushed his cigarette into the ashtray.

'There's just one other matter I'd like to clear up,' he began stifly. 'That money my father left you——'

'I never touched a cent of it,' she interrupted him in a voice that was cold with distaste.

'My God!' he groaned, sitting down heavily on the sofa behind him with his hands hanging limply between his knees.

She had never seen him look so utterly dejected before, but she steeled herself against the growing desire to comfort him, and told him the cold, hard facts. 'I tried to give it back to you, but there were so many legal reasons why I couldn't do so that I finally told the attorney that I had no interest in the money, and that he could do with it what he wished. I'm sure that if you contacted him he would be able to tell you more than I could, since I returned all his correspondence unopened.'

'My God!' Kyle said again, and as they stared at each other they both realised that the past suddenly lay between them like a deep ravine which neither of them was able to cross.

Uncovering the truth had opened up old wounds, and had made a few new ones to erect a barrier between them that seemed immovable. Tricia felt immensely tired as she sat there facing him, knowing that this was yet another of those days she would never forget. There had been so many such days in her life since knowing him, and each one of them brought forth its own particular pain.

'I'll make us something to drink,' she murmured when the silence between them became unbearable and, bending forward to retrieve her empty cup, she felt something slither from the neck of her sweater, and to her horror found herself staring at the silver falcon swinging free on its chain about her throat.

Leaving her cup where it was, she straightened quickly and turned from Kyle, but he was beside her in an instant, his hand closing about the silver charm before she could return it to its hiding place. Fear rendered her immobile, and when he opened his hand she stared fixedly at the charm lying against his palm.

'I remember when I gave you this,' he remarked softly. 'You said then that you would always wear it because it reminded you of me. Remember?'

Her heart was beating out a wild tattoo, and her throat felt curiously dry as she whispered hoarsely, 'I remember.'

'Is it possible that—despite everything—you still —care?' he asked in a strange, halting voice.

'Please, Kyle,' she begged unsteadily.

'No, don't turn away,' he ordered with some

urgency, releasing the charm to frame her face between his strong hands. 'Look at me, Tricia, and answer me truthfully. I *must* know.'

His eyes probed hers; probed deeply as if to penetrate her very soul, and fearing what he might see, she lowered her lashes and said quickly, 'It's too late, Kyle.'

'It's never too late if you——'

'No!' she cried hoarsely, thrusting him from her with unexpected strength and walking across to the open window to draw several deep breaths of air into her lungs in an effort to steady herself before she could trust herself to face him again. 'Kyle ... I'm going to marry Frank Carlson.'

His eyes narrowed with arrogant disbelief. 'You can't seriously still consider marrying him?'

'There's nothing to consider. I'm going to marry him.'

'Does he know about us, and——'

'He knows everything.'

His eyebrows rose fractionally. 'And he still wants to marry you, knowing everything as he does?'

A sudden spurt of anger made her raise her chin defiantly. 'He loves me.'

'Meaning I don't?' Kyle returned with a hint of renewed mockery in his eyes.

'Meaning that I gave my word, and I have no intention of breaking it.'

'Because you love him?'

'That's none of your business,' she snapped angrily.

'It is my business,' he informed her harshly, his lips tightening ominously. 'You can't sacrifice your own happiness in this way.'

'I don't consider marrying Frank a sacrifice,' she retorted defensively. 'He's the kind, dependable sort, and he's always been good to me in the past. I know I shall enjoy a happy, stable life with him. I've made my choice.'

CHAPTER EIGHT

KYLE'S mocking laughter echoed round the room. 'A happy, stable life,' he repeated after her with a cynicism that made her flinch inwardly as if he had struck her. 'Is that what you really want, Tricia? A comfortable but dreary life with a man who will never acquire the ability to kindle those hidden fires in you?'

Her cheeks grew hot and she clutched at the windowsill behind her for support when her heart began to beat erratically against her ribs. 'You don't know what you're talking about!'

'Don't I?' he demanded, a dangerous sensuality in his smile and in the way he moved as he closed the gap between them and, anticipating her darting movement to the side, his arm shot out, and the next moment she found herself trapped against the wall by the solid length of his body.

Her breasts were hurting against the immovable hardness of his chest, and his ruthless hands were in her hair, forcing her head back until the teasing touch of his lips against her throat sent shivers of unwanted delight rippling through her.

'Don't!' she moaned, trying to twist away from him, but his hands tightened in her hair, and the sharp pain in her scalp halted her struggles more effectively than anything else could have done.

His light, feathery kisses tantalised her as they travelled a path of destruction up to the sensitive hollow behind her ear, and her defences crumbled long before his lips found hers. His mouth moved over hers with a remembered urgency that sharpened her senses and played havoc with her emotions and, as she relaxed against him, his hands moved down her back to her waist, then up again beneath her sweater to cup her swelling breasts.

Ecstasy, sharp and exquisite, surged through her, and she moaned softly, aware now of every hard line of his virile body against her own. Her hands moved of their own volition to become locked behind his head where the hair grew strong and crisp into his neck, but sanity returned and brought with it an acute sense of renewed shame when she felt him draw her purposefully towards the sofa.

'Kyle, please don't!' she cried in a choked voice as she wrenched her mouth from his and, to her relief, his arms fell away from her instantly.

'I've proved something, haven't I,' he stated thickly, beads of perspiration standing out on his forehead while his glance roamed the length of her to linger eventually on the gentle but thrusting swell of her breasts beneath her thin sweater where she could still feel the touch of his caressing hands.

'You've proved nothing except that there's an undeniable physical attraction between us,' she contradicted defiantly, her cheeks flaming and her breathing rapid at the thought of how close she had come to surrendering herself.

'Will it satisfy you to always have only the surface of your emotions skimmed when you know you can reach the heights with me?' he demanded on a note of intimacy that quickened her pulse and sent the blood flowing more swiftly through her veins.

'No, it won't always satisfy me!' she wanted to cry out, but she looked away from the devastation of his tawny gaze and swallowed down the bitterness of her disappointment. She wanted love; Kyle spoke of desire. Not once during their entire relationship had he mentioned the word 'love', and she came to the hateful conclusion that he had nothing of offer her except an affair which might be sexually satisfying to them both, but never binding or lasting. A moment ago she had been tempted to relinquish her decision to marry Frank, but now she knew what she had to do and, raising her glance no higher than his square jaw, she said firmly, 'I've already committed myself, Kyle, and I can't go back on my word.'

She saw his mouth tighten while a paleness seeped beneath his deeply tanned skin, and then she turned away, afraid that he would see her quivering lips, and the utter desolation mirrored in her dark eyes while they rapidly filled with tears.

'I'm returning to Cape Town tomorrow,' he stated in cold, decisive tones, and although she had known that he would soon be leaving, it came as a shock to learn how soon. 'If you should change your mind,' he added abruptly, 'you'll know where to find me.'

The room swam before her eyes as she heard him walk away, but it was only when she heard him close the door firmly behind him that she gave way to the choking sobs that rose in her throat. There in the lounge, with Kyle's presence still lingering so prominently in the air, she wept long and bitter tears until she felt certain she had been drained of every scrap of emotion.

She slept that night from sheer exhaustion, and awoke on the Saturday morning with a throbbing headache which lingered on through until lunch time. Frank took her out to dinner that evening, and although she made a supreme effort to appear normal in his company, her powers of conversation seemed to have deserted her, and long, unnatural silences began to settle between them with the result that Frank glanced at her more than once with a worried frown between his dark brows. The food was excellent, and so was the wine, but she did not have the stamina to conjure up an enthusiasm she did not feel, and she was intensely relieved when Frank suggested that he take her home.

When they arrived at her flat she invited him in for a cup of coffee and they listened to one of their favourite records, but later, when he drew her into his arms and kissed her, she leaned against him wearily and wished, for the first time, that he would not be so gentle with her.

'You seem troubled, Tricia?' he said at last, drawing a little away from her. 'You've been very quiet all evening,' he added, 'and that isn't like you at all.'

'Nothing is troubling me,' she lied guiltily, going back into his arms. 'Just hold me, and kiss me.'

His arms tightened about her, but his kiss remained gentle and controlled as if he was afraid of bruising her lips. Kyle's mocking face swam before her eyes, and out of sheer desperation she locked her hands behind Frank's head and drew it down further, increasing the pressure of his mouth on her now parted lips. Their kiss deepened, but it took every scrap of feeling she possessed to respond to him in that manner while she knew, deep down, that the most vital spark was missing.

She could feel his thudding heart against her breasts, and his breathing was rapid as he whispered into her ear, 'I love you so much, Tricia.'

'I know,' she murmured with an ache in her heart, resigning herself with difficulty to what the future held in store for her. 'I know you love me.'

They kissed again, but this time the effort to respond was a little too much for Tricia, and Frank was quick to sense the change in her.

'You're tired,' he smiled down at her, brushing a dark curl behind her shell-like ear as if she were a little girl. 'Go to bed, and sleep late tomorrow. I'll see you after lunch, and if you feel up to it, we might take a drive out somewhere into the country.'

Tricia felt better on Sunday, but still she could not bring herself to talk to Frank about what had occurred. It was all still too new and too painful to even bear thinking about.

At the office on the Monday morning, she flung herself into her work in a relentless effort to stave off her thoughts, and her pencil seemed to fly over the paper when she took down the letters David McGregor dictated.

He leaned back in his chair eventually, and smiled that slow, boyish smile she was beginning to know. 'I don't know about you, but I prefer working without the chief breathing fire down my neck.'

Her laughter surprised even herself, then she asked self-consciously, 'How long have you been working for Mr Hammond?'

'I joined the staff of Union Timber directly after leaving university, so that makes it two years.' He lit a cigarette and blew the smoke rather impatiently through his nose. 'I was told that his father had been just such a dragon when he sat in the chair Kyle now occupies.'

'He may have been a dragon,' she smiled reminiscently, 'But Benjamin Hammond was also very kind, and extremely sensitive to someone else's needs.'

'You knew him?' David McGregor wanted to know, his eyes suddenly alert and infinitely curious.

'Yes, I knew him,' she admitted, but as he leaned forward in his chair to question her further, she hastily changed the subject. 'When do you expect the building operations to start on the new premises?'

'Next month.' He drew hard on his cigarette and relaxed in his chair once more. 'You'll be leaving our employ before the builders arrive, I believe.'

His reminder sent a stab of pain through her, but threaded through it was a deep nostalgia for the old and familiar things which would soon no longer be there. 'Yes, I shall be gone before they arrive.'

'I'm sorry about that,' he remarked with a rueful smile. 'Efficient secretaries are rather difficult to find.'

'You flatter me, Mr McGregor.'

'David, remember?' His smile deepened, then receded with equal swiftness. 'Could you recommend anyone to replace you?'

'Miss Usher from the accounts department has all the necessary qualifications,' she replied calmly and without hesitation, while the only sign of mental stress was in the way her hands tightened on her notebook and pencil. 'She used to take over from me whenever I went away on holiday.'

'Miss Usher, you say,' he muttered, picking up his pen and scribbling down the name on his jotter. 'Get her file for me, and ask her to come up and see me immediately after lunch this afternoon, will you?'

'Certainly.'

Tricia found Rosalie Usher's file in the cabinet and placed it on his desk, but when she returned to her own office she sat down behind her typewriter and closed her eyes for a moment to collect her scattered thoughts before she telephoned down to the accounts department.

'What's it all about, Tricia?' Rosalie Usher wanted to know when she entered Tricia's office after lunch that day. 'Why does the boss want to see me?'

Tricia looked up at the slim, fair-haired girl who was four years her junior, and explained, 'Mr McGregor is hoping to find someone who could take my place. I'm leaving at the end of the month.'

The girl relaxed visibly, and smiled. 'So you've finally made up your mind to marry Frank, have you?'

Tricia returned the smile a little tightly, and flicked the switch on the intercom. 'Miss Usher is here to see you, Mr McGregor.'

'Send her in, please,' David McGregor's voice crackled over the intercom, and Tricia gestured Rosalie towards the door.

'Wish me luck,' the girl whispered, and then the door closed behind her.

Alone once more, Tricia brushed aside her depressing thoughts and concentrated on her work, but she could not prevent herself from wondering whether she had, after all, made a wise decision to marry Frank. Her fingers paused momentarily in their flight across the typewriter keys, and she lowered her glance to the cluster of diamonds on her finger. It was too late now for doubts, she scolded herself silently, then she gave her complete attention to her work.

Rosalie came out of David McGregor's office a half hour later, and Tricia looked up enquiringly as the girl approached her desk. 'Well? Do I congratulate you?'

'Yes, I've got the job,' Rosalie smiled brightly.

'Good.' Tricia drew the sheet of paper out of her typewriter and placed it neatly in the folder on her desk. 'How soon can they release you down in Accounts?'

'Mr McGregor said he would make arrangements for me to come up here as from next Monday.'

'That should give you enough time to acclimatise.'

Rosalie nodded enthusiastically and then gestured with her head towards the inner office. 'He's good-looking, isn't he, but Kyle Hammond was more my style. I've never met a man before who could turn my knees to jelly just by being in the same room with me.'

Tricia knew exactly what she meant, and she smiled faintly. 'You'd better not let your boy-friend hear you say that!'

'Peter's not the jealous type, thank goodness,' Rosalie Usher laughed happily, then she glanced up at the clock. 'I'd better get going, or they might think I've decided to take the entire afternoon off!'

Tricia stared after her with mixed feelings, but the intercom crackled on her desk, and a few moments later she was hurrying through to David McGregor's office with the papers he required.

She was kept too busy during the rest of the week to brood about her future, but it was the nights that she feared most; nights when she would lie awake with her thoughts for company, and with very little hope of getting sufficient rest. More than once she was tempted to take a sleeping tablet for relief in oblivion, but fear of becoming addicted to it prevented her from doing so, with the result that she was up before dawn most mornings, tidying her flat, and forcing herself to eat something before she went out to work.

It was on the Wednesday of the following week that Charles Barrett telephoned her unexpectedly at the office, and she could have wept for joy at the sound of his gravelly voice.

'What about coming out to Buffalo Bay and spending the weekend with us?' he suggested after enquiring after her health.

'I would love to,' she said at once, 'but wouldn't it be inconvenient for you to have me?'

'Don't be silly, child,' Charles laughed good-naturedly, and then she could distinguish a woman's voice in the background moments before Charles said: 'Here's Milly. She will convince you if I can't.'

'Tricia?' Milly Barrett's warm familiar voice came over the line. 'We're missing all our old friends, and we would really love to have you, my dear. Do come along on Friday afternoon after work if you can manage it. There's plenty of room, and

I'm dying to show off our new home.'

'I shall look forward to seeing it now that you've settled in,' Tricia said eventually, succumbing to the temptation of a weekend at their cottage at Buffalo Bay.

'That's settled, then,' Milly said happily. 'See you on Friday.'

Tricia had begun to pack her small weekend suitcase on the Thursday evening when Frank telephoned to say he would be leaving early the following morning for Port Elizabeth to collect the car parts he had ordered. He did not expect to return to Knysna before the Monday afternoon, he added, and she felt strangely relieved at the news as it made it easier for her then to tell him of her intention to spend the weekend with Charles and Milly Barrett.

When their conversation ended, she experienced an odd sensation of freedom; freedom to do as she wished, if only for a weekend, and she reacted impulsively by removing the cumbersome engagement ring from her finger and locking it away safely. Her thoughts were in a turmoil, and she needed time to consider her actions before she told Charles and Milly about her engagement to Frank.

Tricia left the office on the Friday afternoon and drove west towards Buffalo Bay with a feeling closely resembling elation. More than a month had gone by since Charles and Milly had left Knysna, but it had felt like an eternity, and she looked forward to seeing them again. She had almost an hour of daylight left for the twenty-one-kilometre drive to their cottage, and she settled behind the wheel of her green Citroën. She knew the way, for she had been to Buffalo Bay once before, and the directions

Charles had given her before their departure from Knysna had been most explicit.

At the Goukamma river, where the arum lilies grew in wild profusion along the roadside, Tricia left the main road and turned off to the left towards the bay, and fifteen minutes later she was parked outside their thatched cottage, with Charles and Milly hurrying down the stone-flagged path to welcome her.

The few weeks without the stress and strain of work had already done wonders for her former employer, Tricia noticed at once, and Milly, slender for her years, was still the warm, sincere person she had always been. Taking her suitcase from her, they ushered her through the gate along the path with its border of yellow daisies towards the front door with its ornamental brass knocker, and in the excitement she caught only a further brief glimpse of a neat green lawn and late autumn roses before she found herself in the spacious but cosy interior of their new home.

Milly had selected warm colours and comfortable furniture to suit the atmosphere of the cottage, but several familiar objects had remained; such as the tall grandfather clock which had been in the Barrett family for years, and the porcelain Siamese cat above the fireplace which still seemed to smile at Tricia in that benign way.

Tricia followed Milly through to the room which had been prepared for her while Charles poured out their sherry and, as she looked about her with interest, taking in the pale lemon and olive-green decor, she felt the tension of the past few days uncoil slowly within her.

'Have you been overdoing things lately?' Milly asked, studying Tricia closely, and her shrewd glance glimpsed the guarded look that leapt into those dark brown eyes moments before long dark lashes swept down to hide their expression. 'Have you, Tricia?'

'Not really, why?'

'You've lost weight, and I don't like the look of those dark smudges beneath your eyes.'

Tricia knew she could not keep the truth from her for long, but she made a pretence of straightening the scarf about her neck and said evasively, 'I haven't been sleeping too well lately.'

'And not eating too well either, I think,' Milly laughed goodnaturedly, 'but that shall be remedied this weekend. I've planned all your favourite dishes.'

'You've always spoiled me, Milly,' Tricia smiled, grateful that the older woman did not delve too deeply into the reason for her loss of weight and lacklustre appearance.

'Since I have no daughter of my own, it's been my privilege,' Milly replied to Tricia's statement, and the glow of warmth that spread through Tricia made her eyes fill with tears. Milly was quick to notice their unnatural brightness and, linking her arm comfortingly through Tricia's, she said smilingly, 'Come along, my dear. Charles always gets agitated when he's kept waiting.'

After a superb dinner that evening they sat in the living-room and talked until well after eleven before going to bed, and that night, for the first time in two weeks, Tricia slept dreamlessly, not waking until Milly brought a tray of breakfast into her the following morning and announced that it was eight-thirty.

'When you've had your breakfast, you might like to take a stroll down to the beach,' Milly suggested, watching with satisfaction as Tricia tucked into the fruit juice, bacon and eggs which had been prepared for her. 'The walk will do you the world of good, and you may find Charles down there somewhere,' she added, turning towards the door, 'but make sure that you're both back in time for tea.'

Tricia leaned back against the pillows, and her contemplative frown gave way to a lazy smile. Milly's suggestion, that she should go for a walk, had sounded almost like an order, but it was an order which she was only too willing to obey.

Dressed warmly in slacks, a thick woollen sweater, and sturdy shoes, Tricia took a brisk walk down to the beach after breakfast, and drew the fresh, tangy sea air deep into her lungs. There was a chill in the breeze as it whipped the dark strands of hair about her face, but she did not care. The sand was soft beneath her feet, and she paused for a moment where the wild flowers grew in splendid profusion on the sand dunes, stopping impulsively to finger the tiny bright yellow petals.

A seagull screeched and swooped low above her head, but, as she looked up to follow its flight, she caught sight of Charles waving to her from the rocks further along the beach. She waved back at once, and made her way towards him across the sand, thankful for her sturdy shoes when she finally picked her precarious way over the ragged rocks to where Charles was seated.

They sat and talked for some time with the roar

of the sea in their ears. She told him about David McGregor, and of the changes that were to take place at the mill, deliberately steering the conversation into an impersonal direction until, suddenly, there was nothing left to say. She narrowed her eyes against the sun and watched the fleecy clouds chasing each other across the blue sky while they changed shape and form with a restlessness that matched her own thoughts.

'What's troubling you, Tricia?'

Startled, she glanced quickly at Charles, and then away again to where the waves were breaking further along the beach, and sending up a spray of foam into the air. She should have known that Charles and Milly knew her much too well to be fooled for any great length of time by her artificial brightness and, sighing, she picked up a small piece of driftwood and prodded listlessly at a small crevice beside her feet.

'I'm going to marry Frank,' she said at last, and another lengthy silence followed before Charles finally spoke.

'I know I should congratulate you, Tricia, but somehow you don't sound very happy about the decision you have made.'

'I'm not quite sure how I feel about it myself,' she admitted with a self-conscious laugh.

'I think you'd better explain,' Charles suggested quietly, cupping his hand about the flame of his lighter as he lit a cigarette.

'I said I would marry Frank because I—I was afraid,' she confessed.

'Afraid of Kyle?' he asked bluntly, his eyebrows rising fractionally in surprise.

'Of what he could do to me, yes.'

'So you agreed to become engaged to Frank because such an engagement could offer you the necessary protection against Kyle.'

Tricia looked up suddenly and met the steady regard of his grey eyes. 'Said like that it sounds awful, I know.'

'And isn't it?'

Taken aback, she lowered her glance hastily, then a wry smile curved her mouth. 'You never did believe in mincing words, did you?'

'It's never any good trying to elude the truth, no matter how ugly it is,' Charles stated firmly, and all at once she was placed on the defensive.

'I'm very fond of Frank. I respect him, and I think that, given a chance, we could be very happy together.'

'Then why are you doubting your decision?' Charles demanded, slapping the ball right back into her own court with an unexpected ruthlessness.

She stared at him speechlessly for a moment before she looked away, her haunted eyes resting on the fishing vessels anchored far out at sea. Then she said with inherent truthfulness, 'Perhaps I'm doubting my decision now that Kyle has discovered the truth.'

'I see,' Charles murmured with growing understanding while he stared thoughtfully at the tip of his cigarette. 'Did you tell him?'

'No,' she shook her head slightly and flung the piece of driftwood back into the sea. 'Kyle tricked Maxine into giving herself away.'

'I never imagined she would tell the truth willingly, but I never thought she would allow herself to be tricked into it either,' Charles observed dryly.

Tricia wrenched her mind from the visions it conjured up of that dreadful afternoon two weeks ago, and said hastily, 'I don't want to go into detail about how it happened, but Kyle is now aware that Maxine was entirely responsible for his father's death.'

Charles regarded her closely for a moment, and then he asked quietly, 'Do you still love him?'

This straight-to-the-shoulder questioning was typical of Charles Barrett, but she stubbornly refused to give him the answer he desired. 'I gave Frank my word I would marry him,' she replied evasively.

Charles drew hard on his cigarette and flicked the remainder into the sea with an exasperated expression on his wrinkled face. 'I'm not concerned with Frank at the moment. I asked if you still loved Kyle.'

Her quivering lips gave him the answer long before she finally relented. 'Yes, I do still love him,' she whispered. 'But——'

'And how does Kyle feel about you?' Charles rapped out the next question before she could complete her sentence.

'I . . . don't know,' she replied slowly, fighting against the tears which threatened to choke her. 'He wanted me, I know, and he seemed to be angered at the thought that I could still contemplate marrying Frank, but he never actually offered marriage himself.'

'What did he suggest, then? An affair?'

'Not in so many words, no, but that's the conclusion I eventually came to, that he was offering me the thrill of an affair, and nothing more.'

Charles observed her in silence for a moment while she picked up a piece of seaweed and fingered it agitatedly, then he asked, 'What would you have done if he'd asked you to marry him?'

'I couldn't marry him now!' she replied at once with a measure of distaste.

'Because of everything that has happened between you?' he wanted to know.

'No, it isn't that at all,' she corrected swiftly, steadying her quivering lower lip between her teeth before she confessed truthfully, 'It's Frank. He loves me, and I couldn't hurt him now by—by calling off our marriage.'

'Do you think it's fair of you to marry Frank without loving him?'

'Am I being fair to myself by continuing to wait and hope for something I know I could never have? Am I being unfair in wanting to take what little happiness life may have to offer me?' she demanded in an anguished voice, and then, as the tears spilled over on to her cheeks, she buried her face in her hands and wept. 'Oh, lord, I wish I knew what to do about the mess my life is in!'

Charles placed a comforting arm about her shoulders and, pressing a clean handkerchief into her hands, he allowed her to cry against his fatherly shoulder. When at last her weeping ceased he said gently, 'I can't tell you what to do, Tricia, but I would advise strongly that you don't consider entering into a marriage with Frank unless you're absolutely certain in your own mind that that's what you want.'

'I wonder if I shall ever be completely sure,

but ...' She paused to wipe her eyes and blow her nose, feeling much better now that she had talked to Charles, but the smile she gave him was still far from steady. 'Thank you for listening, and I—I'll give the matter a great deal more thought.'

'Come along,' he smiled, hugging her briefly. 'My throat is dry, and I think Milly must have tea waiting for us.'

After that heart-to-heart talk with Charles, she managed to shelve her problems for the duration of the weekend until Milly entered her room on the Sunday afternoon while she was putting her things together for her return trip to Knysna.

'I've been wanting to have a little private talk with you, Tricia,' she began a little hesitantly, seating herself on the corner of the bed. 'I know we've discussed your engagement to Frank at great length, but there's something I want to say to you; something I couldn't say in front of Charles.' She paused a little uncertainly, then she drew Tricia down beside her, and her glance was faintly reminiscent when she continued to speak. 'When a man isn't wholly in love with the woman he marries, the marriage could still succeed, but when a *woman* doesn't wholly love the man she marries, the marriage has very little chance of lasting. Marriage, to a man, is very much a physical thing, but to a woman it's much more than that. She must love with her heart as well as her soul before she gives herself to the man of her choice.' She met Tricia's questioning glance, and her smile was tinged with remembered sadness as she explained, 'The girl Charles hoped to marry died a few weeks before I met him. After a time we discovered that we enjoyed each other's company, and I soon fell in love with him. When Charles eventually asked me to marry him, I knew he didn't love me as I would have wished, but through the years my love reached out to him until I finally succeeded in winning his love and respect.' There was now a certain urgency in the hands that clasped Tricia's as Milly added: 'A woman who loves has the patience to wait, and the ingenuity to work at her marriage to achieve what she wants, but a man may grow tired and bored with a wife who doesn't love him, and that's when the marriage begins to crumble.'

Tricia found it difficult to believe that Charles and Milly were ever anything other than deeply in love with each other, but during the silence that followed Milly's disclosure, she began to feel a little uneasy.

'Are you trying to tell me it would be a mistake for me to marry Frank?' she asked hesitantly.

'I would never presume to interfere in your life to such an extent, but I would like you to promise me, my dear, that you'll give the matter very serious thought before you decide finally.' Milly's glance was filled with concern. 'Charles and I both know that Frank is a wonderful man, and that he would make some woman an excellent husband, but be very sure that *you* want to be that woman.'

Tricia considered this for a moment, and then she said gravely, 'Thank you for telling me what you have, and I promise I'll think it over very carefully before I find myself in a position where it's too late to change my mind.'

'Good,' Milly sighed, looking considerably relieved. 'We want you to be happy, Tricia, because we feel no one deserves happiness more than you do.'

'Bless you, Milly,' she whispered, swallowing down the lump which had risen in her throat. 'And thank you.'

When Tricia drove back to Knysna that afternoon she found that the few days she had spent with Charles and Milly had given her a considerable amount to think about. In their own inimitable way they had tried to help her, but the final decision would still have to be her own, and she knew that it would not be an easy decision to make. Could she hurt someone she cared for when the existing situation had been created initially by her own thoughtless and selfish actions? Tricia was not so sure that she could. Her actions at the time had been motivated by an unreasonable fear; a fear which had now dwindled into insignificance, but that was no longer an acceptable excuse for what she had done. She had used Frank in a shameful manner, and yet she had truly believed that they could be happy together. Part of her still believed this, but, after talking to Charles and Milly, there was a part of her that was beginning to think differently.

CHAPTER NINE

TRICIA struggled through the following week with her mind in a turmoil of indecision. Time was running out on her at a frightening pace, and still she could not decide what to do. Frank's ring was on her finger, but Kyle was in her heart, and she was torn between her loyalty and fondness for the one, and her inescapable love and yearning for the other. To make matters worse, an unnatural tension had developed in her relationship with Frank, making it impossible for her to relax in his company, and causing her to shrink from him mentally and physically each time he tried to come near her.

'What is it, Tricia?' he demanded angrily one evening when she had avoided his arms not for the first time since his arrival at her flat.

'I don't know what you mean,' she said guardedly, deliberately playing for time, but guilt stained her cheeks a delicate pink and then receded swiftly to leave her pale.

'My dear, I know you better than you think,' Frank explained with forced calmness. 'Ever since Kyle Hammond returned to Cape Town, leaving that other chap in command, you've been behaving oddly, and I want to know what it is. Have you changed your mind about marrying me?'

'Frank, it isn't . . .' She paused as their eyes met, and the directness of his gaze made her realise that she could no longer withhold the facts from him.

'Kyle has discovered the truth about his father's death,' she said at last.

His rugged features remained expressionless except for the slight tightening of his lips. 'I think you'd better tell me about it.'

She sat down wearily in the armchair facing him and, succeeding in keeping her voice calm and controlled, she related every detail of that afternoon when Maxine had stormed uninvited into Kyle's office, but she found she could not tell him of Kyle's visit to her flat that evening.

Frank listened to her quietly without interrupting, and when she fell silent he sat for a long time staring down at his tightly-clenched work-roughened hands before he said roughly, 'It's still Kyle, isn't it?'

The pained expression on his face was too much for her, and she said anxiously, 'Oh, let's forget about Kyle!'

'I can,' he assured her hastily with unfamiliar cynicism. 'Can you?'

'No! Never!' the words flashed across her mind, but she bit them back forcibly before they tumbled from her lips and instead she said resolutely, 'I did agree to marry you, Frank.'

'Because you love me, or because you're afraid of being hurt again?'

These words dealt a shattering blow to her conscience, but before she could think of a suitable reply he was drawing her to her feet and into his arms. He kissed her in a way he had never done before, bruising her lips as he forced them apart with his own, while his hands caressed her body with an intimacy he had never dared to seek before. She did not recoil physically from his touch, and remained perfectly still, desperately willing herself to respond to his lovemaking, but she realised then that nothing could have shown her more clearly what a dreadful mistake she would be making if she persisted in her decision to marry this man.

An eternity seemed to pass before his arms fell away from her and, stepping back, he smiled a little twistedly. 'You've tried very hard to love me, my dear, but you know as well as I do that it's no use, is it?'

She looked away, unable to bear the pain in his eyes, and the guilty knowledge that she had put it there. 'Frank, I—I'm very fond of you, and I—I honestly thought we could make a success of our marriage, but——'

'Kyle would always have been there between us, the unseen third party in our marriage,' Frank interrupted with a bitterness that stung her.

Her eyes filled with tears, but she blinked them back quickly. 'Frank, I'm sorry, I——'

'I'm setting you free, Tricia,' he sighed, gripping her shoulders with unsteady hands. 'Go to Kyle, my dear, if that's what you want, but God help him if he makes you unhappy.'

His hands tightened momentarily on her shoulders, then he put her aside and was striding from the room. She stood motionless for a moment, as if her feet had been nailed to the floor, then she ran after him and caught up with him as he reached the door.

'Frank!'

He turned at once. 'Yes, my dear?'

She tried desperately to think of something to

say: something to alleviate the pain and misery she glimpsed in his eyes, but she finally relinquished the effort and, slipping his ring off her finger, she placed it in his hand.

'Forgive me,' she said simply, but her voice was wavery and thick with tears.

His fingers caressed her cheek lightly, and then he was gone, leaving her with the unpleasant feeling that yet another chapter in her life had come to an end, and in the process, she had lost a very dear and wonderful friend.

Rosalie Usher was quick to notice the following morning that Tricia's hand was free of its usual adornment, but it was not until they took time off to have their tea that she asked inquisitively, 'What happened to your ring?'

'Frank and I decided last night that it would be the best thing for both of us if we discontinued with our engagement,' Tricia informed her calmly while she sipped at her tea.

'But why?' Rosalie demanded incredulously. 'You've known each other for so many years.'

'Perhaps that's why we realised it wouldn't work,' Tricia said evasively.

Rosalie drank her tea thirstily and poured herself a second cup before she asked curiously, 'What happens now?'

'I work my notice, and ...' Tricia paused and shrugged. 'Who knows?'

The younger girl's fingers seemed to fidget with the teaspoon in her saucer, and Tricia suspected the reason for her discomfiture even before she spoke.

'I have no intention of withdrawing my resignation, Rosalie,' she forestalled her hastily. 'I think I might be leaving Knysna, but I haven't decided finally yet.'

'Where will you go?' Rosalie wanted to know, making an effort to hide her relief, but not quite succeeding.

Tricia shrugged again. 'There's a possibility that I might settle in Cape Town, but I haven't given the matter much thought. Perhaps I'll take a holiday first, and decide afterwards.'

'I've never known you in such an undecided mood,' Rosalie commented after a lengthy pause, and Tricia glanced at her in surprise.

'Quite frankly, Rosalie,' she said with a faint smile hovering about her mouth, 'I'm a stranger to myself lately.'

Rosalie did not question her further on the subject, but as the time drew near for Tricia to leave Barrett's she often recalled Rosalie's remark concerning her indecision.

She had not seen Frank at all since that night he had set her free. She missed his company dreadfully at times, but she realised they could not go on seeing each other under the existing circumstances. She needed to be alone to think, and to decide one way or the other where her future lay, but with only a few working days left to her she was still caught up in a web of indecision.

'What *am* I going to do?' she asked herself one night when the future loomed desolately before her. Kyle had said that if she should change her mind she would know where to find him, but he had given her no indication as to what she could expect if she should follow him up on his rather dubious invitation. Would he offer her marriage, or expect her to become his mistress? Could she go to him and say, 'Here I am. Take me for what I'm worth, and do with me what you please.' Dared she risk it? she wondered nervously.

Her mind said 'no', but her heart said 'yes', and from the debris of their silent battle the answer emerged quite clearly. Six long years of separation had not stilled her love for Kyle. Instead of dwindling, it had grown richer and stronger, and despite the unhappiness she had suffered, or might still suffer in the future because of him, she would go on loving him until she breathed her last breath.

'I'll go to him,' she decided finally. 'If he'll have me, I'll accept whatever he has to offer, and I shall cherish it for as long as I am able.'

It was with a curious feeling of resignation that Tricia went to bed that night, but during her last few days at work she found herself caught up in a whirl of nervous excitement at the thought of seeing Kyle again. Her listlessness and indecision vanished like mist before the sun, and she was well aware of Rosalie Usher and David McGregor's curious glances, but a tiny flicker of doubt, which she constantly had to suppress, forced her to remain silent.

'What are your plans for the future,' David McGregor wanted to know from her when she had accepted a silver tea service from him as a going-away gift from the staff.

'I haven't made any definite plans yet,' Tricia replied carefully, dabbing at her moist eyes with her handkerchief, 'but I'll let you know.'

'Take a long holiday,' Rosalie suggested, 'and be

sure to send us a postcard.'

'I'll do that,' Tricia smiled shakily, hoping feverishly that, if things worked out satisfactorily for her, she would be able to supplement 'holiday' with 'honeymoon'.

Tricia drove away from the mill that Wednesday afternoon for the last time with a feeling of nostalgia, but there were more urgent matters that needed her attention. She was filled with an aching longing and impatience to see Kyle, and to know, once and for all, where she stood.

She knew Kyle's home address in Cape Town, as well as his telephone number, and she had been tempted on several occasions to give him a call, but each time she had decided against it. The telephone was such an impersonal instrument of communication at times, and what had to be said between them could wait until she was there.

She slept very little that night, which was understandable, and she was up before sunrise the following morning. She had several things to do before attempting the long drive to Cape Town and, with luck, she could get away before lunch, she thought as she buttered a thin slice of toast and poured herself a cup of black coffee.

It was one o'clock, however, before she managed to get away, and, to her annoyance, it had started to rain. Was it a bad omen? she wondered with vague uneasiness, but she thrust the thought aside and drove steadily westwards towards Cape Town.

Tricia stopped twice along the way to fill up the car's tank, and once, when darkness fell, to quell the hunger pains that racked her insides. She still had at least another two hours of travelling ahead of her, she calculated roughly, and if it rained any harder she could be assured of an extra hour on the road, she thought dismally as she paid for her meal and pulled her coat more firmly about her before walking out into the rain to where she had parked her car. She disliked travelling after dark and, with the rain hampering her visibility, she began to wonder if she should not have stayed over somewhere for the night, but the thought of having to live through another night of uncertainty made her grit her teeth and push on relentlessly towards her destination.

It was after eight that evening when Tricia finally arrived in Rondebosch, Cape Town's most exclusive suburb. It was still raining heavily, with the result that it took her some minutes to find the street she was searching for, but by this time it felt as though her heart was pounding in her mouth, and the doubts, which she had kept at bay since making her decision, came rushing in to torment her. What if she had made a mistake? What if Kyle had not been serious, and she had been fool enough to take him at his word? What if he no longer wanted her?

In a blind panic, her foot went down on the accelerator, and the Citroën shot forward at the precise moment that a large black dog chose to cross the street. There was no time to contemplate her actions and, putting her foot down hard on the brake pedal, she swung the car to the left, narrowly missing the dog as well as skimming past the gnarled stem of a tree to come to a shuddering stop centimetres from a broad white pillar marking the entrance to a long, curved driveway.

She had no idea what had happened to the dog, although she was certain of having missed him, but, as tremors of shock rippled through her body, she rested her arms on the steering wheel and buried her white face in them. It took her several seconds to pull herself together, but a second shock awaited her when she raised her head slowly and stared out through the windscreen. The white pillar she had almost rammed her car into stood at the entrance to Kyle's home, and when she started the car to reverse it out of the shallow ditch, the rear wheels merely spun themselves deeper into the mud. It was too late to think of retreat, and she was left with no other alternative but to walk up the long drive towards the house, hoping and praying that if the reception she received was not the one she had hoped for, then she could at least expect some assistance in getting her car out of the ditch.

Tricia climbed out stiffly and shivered as she locked the car, then, buttoning up her coat to keep out the rain and the cold, she walked up the tarred driveway, skipping across puddles of water until she was within sight of the pillared entrance to the large, two-storied mansion which had stood half hidden behind the trees. The lights were on in several of the downstairs rooms, she noticed when she paused momentarily beneath a tree for shelter from the driving rain. The warm, dry interior of the house beckoned her, but she stood rooted to the spot with indecision and nervousness. Was she on the verge of making a fool of herself, or had Kyle been sincere?

The raindrops trickling from her hair down into her neck assisted her in making up her mind swiftly and, taking a deep, steadying breath, she sprinted across the remaining distance towards the sheltered front door. Her hand went out towards the brass knocker, but hovered there nervously without touching it.

'Coward!' she admonished herself loudly and, summoning up the right amount of courage, she raised the knocker and brought it down heavily a few times.

The door opened almost at once, and a white-coated manservant gestured her respectfully into the large, brightly-lit entrance hall.

'Is—Is Mr Hammond in?' she asked hesitantly, coming close to wishing that the reply would be in the negative.

'Mr Hammond is in, madam,' he informed her courteously with a curiously expressionless face as if feminine callers at that time of the evening were a regular occurrence. 'Shall I take your coat?'

She took off her damp coat and he hung it up on an old antique stand in the hall before he ushered her into the living-room where an electric fire burned welcomingly in the grate.

'Who shall I say is calling, madam?'

'Meredith,' she supplied her name. 'Miss Tricia Meredith.'

He bowed slightly and retreated, and then she was left alone to cross the room towards the fireplace where she kneeled to warm her hands while she looked about her with interest.

Above the stone fireplace hung a life-size portrait of Benjamin Hammond. It was the first thing which had drawn her attention on entering the room and, as she looked up into that lean face to find those pale grey eyes smiling down at her, she could almost feel his presence beside her; a kindly, warm presence that gave her a certain amount of courage to face what lay before her.

Arranged about the room were several large, comfortably padded armchairs which were upholstered in a serviceable beige material, while the drapes at the windows were a mixture of deep yellow and golden brown to add a touch of brightness to an otherwise sombre room. Once, perhaps, it had been a room that was lived in, but Tricia doubted very much if Kyle had spent many hours in it during the past years.

The sound of footsteps in the hall made her rise and turn apprehensively to face the door. Outwardly she looked calm and composed, but inwardly her stomach muscles had begun to coil themselves into a painful knot. 'This is it!' she told herself nervously, and the next moment Kyle stood framed in the doorway. In her distracted state he seemed to be taller and leaner, and her heart was pounding so fast that she could hardly breathe, then he stepped further into the living-room, and she saw for the first time that he was not alone. A tall, elegantly dressed brunette, with attractive almond-shaped eyes, followed him into the room, and Tricia glimpsed the smile that curved the woman's full, sensuous mouth as she exchanged a quick glance with Kyle.

Tricia's heart took a sickening downward plunge, and then everything within her seemed to come to a grinding halt. The room swayed about her and, clutching at the mantelshelf for support, she heard herself say in a remarkably steady, but emotionless voice, 'It seems I've arrived at an inopportune moment.'

An odd little silence followed her remark; a silence during which Kyle and this woman exchanged another quick, faintly amused glance, but Tricia no longer cared. She felt incredibly tired, and she was only too aware that her appearance left much to be desired. Her slacks were wet below the knees, and the soles of her shoes were uncomfortably damp, but when a drop of water trickled from her hair on to her nose, she felt like weeping for no other reason except that she had once again been such a gullible idiot. She brushed the raindrop away with the tips of her fingers and, raising her head proudly, faced the two people across the room with a touch of defiance in her glance, but Kyle dampened the fire of her rising anger which was directed mainly at herself.

'This is my secretary, Mrs Jean Sadler,' he said, his expression inscrutable as he stepped forward to make the introductions, and only then did Tricia notice the small leather briefcase which the woman held unobtrusively at her side. 'I have to attend an important board meeting tomorrow morning,' Kyle explained, 'and there were a few things I had to sort out before meeting the other members.'

Relief swept through Tricia like a tidal wave as she took the hand the woman extended towards her, but a new, more terrifying realisation was taking possession of her. Kyle had given no indication that he was glad to see her and, meeting the intensity of his tawny glance, she could almost swear that she saw annoyance lurking in the depths of his eyes.

'I—I'm sorry if I'm in the way,' Tricia apologised

self-consciously to no one in particular.

'Goodness, no! *I'm* the one who is in the way,' Jean Sadler laughed easily as she brushed aside Tricia's apology, then she turned to Kyle. 'I'll have those documents typed and waiting for you on your desk in the morning, Mr Hammond.'

'Good,' he said abruptly.

'I'll see myself out,' his secretary announced, gripping her briefcase under her arm as she turned to smile at Tricia. 'It was nice meeting you, Miss Meredith.'

Tricia smiled stiffly as she murmured something appropriate, but when the living-room door closed behind Jean Sadler she found herself alone with Kyle, and facing him warily across the wide expanse of the stone hearth. He stood motionless, a formidable, frightening stranger as his eyes flicked over her coldly, then he turned away and walked towards the teak sideboard at the far end of the room.

'Would you like something to drink? I have an excellent vintage wine I could offer you.'

His cold, impersonal tone of voice struck a chilling note in her heart, and she heard herself stammer, 'I—thank you, y-yes.'

While he stood with his broad back turned towards her she took the opportunity to study him, and her tender glance caressed the silvery hair growing into his strong neck. She longed to go to him, to touch him, but he looked so utterly unapproachable that her courage began to desert her. He turned at that moment, and she averted her glance hastily, looking up only to thank him when he placed a delicate-stemmed glass between her trembling fingers.

She raised the glass to her lips and sipped at the wine. She felt its warmth flow through her chilled body, restoring her courage partly, then she was groping for something to say, *anything* that would break this awful silence between them.

'Your secretary's very attractive,' she said at last for want of anything better to say.

'She's also very married,' he replied in cold, clipped tones.

'I wasn't suggesting——'

Kyle silenced her angry retort with an imperious wave of his hand, then he asked cynically, 'To what do I owe the honour of this visit?'

'I swerved to avoid a dog in the street and landed my car in the ditch at your gate,' she said a little frantically. 'I'm afraid it will have to be towed out.'

He raised a sardonic eyebrow. 'You were just passing through, then, and because of the incident with the dog you were forced to call in for assistance. Is that it?'

'No, of course not,' she replied a little irritably.

'Then I take it that you actually came to see me about something?'

He had lost weight, she noticed absently as she searched his lean face for something that would give her the courage she needed so desperately, but she found nothing and, draining her glass, she placed it carefully on the low table beside her before she faced him again.

'Kyle, you said—the last time we saw each other —you said——' She faltered nervously, unable to continue as she met his stony, detached glance.

'I recall saying a great many things the last time we saw each other, but what, specifically, are you referring to at the moment?'

It was obvious to her now that he was going to make it as difficult as possible for her to explain why she had come and, realising that she could expect no assistance from him, she gathered the remnants of her courage together and said haltingly, 'You said that—that if I should change my mind about—about marrying Frank, then I—I would know where to find you.'

She waited, a smothered feeling in her chest, but his expression remained unaltered as she watched him empty his glass and place it on the mantelshelf. The seconds seemed to pass with every thundering beat of her heart, and her confusion and bewilderment was finally replaced with the suspicion that Kyle's silence meant that she was being rejected. Despair hung like a weighty cloak about her heart and, unable to face him a moment longer, she turned towards the door.

'It seems I—I made a mistake,' she muttered thickly, fighting back the tears of humiliation as she fled from him.

'Just a minute!' Fingers of steel gripped her arm before she had the opportunity to reach the door, and the pain they inflicted was a sweet agony she had not the strength nor the desire to escape from as he drew her shivering form back towards the warmth of the fire. 'What made you change your mind?'

'It—It was Frank, actually, who changed it for me,' she replied haltingly, rubbing her arm gingerly where his fingers had bruised the soft flesh.

'Do you mean he released you from your promise to marry him?'

'Yes.'

'Why?'

'He—he realised that—that it wouldn't work.'

'Could you be a little more explicit?'

Tricia longed to know what this inquisition of Kyle's was leading up to as she said miserably, 'He realised that I was in——' She bit back the rest of her revealing sentence, and hastily corrected herself with, 'He realised that I could never love him in the way he loved me, so he decided to set me free.'

'You were going to say that he realised you were in love with me, not so?' Kyle commented in a dangerously quiet voice and, when embarrassment prevented her from replying, he gripped her shoulders with punishing hands and shook her with unnecessary violence. 'Not so, Tricia?' he demanded now in a harsh voice.

Her head snapped back as a result of his rough treatment, and his probing, searching eyes captured hers relentlessly to delve so deeply beneath the surface of her soul that she began to feel resentful at having her innermost secrets exposed. She wanted to deny his statement, she wanted to lash out and hurt him in the way he was hurting her, but the touch of his hands sent a primitive thrill racing through her veins, and the familiar smell of his masculine cologne filled her nostrils and attacked her senses in the most forceful and delicious way.

She did not want to fight him, she realised with sudden clarity. She wanted to be held in his arms, to feel the hard warmth of his body against her own, and she wanted to lose herself in the magic which only his kiss could provide for her. Her eyes grew misty with the force of her own emotions, while a familiar weakness invaded her limbs, and as he shook her again, demanding the truth which she had been so reluctant to give, she sagged limply against him until her head fell forward on to his broad chest.

'Yes, yes, yes!' she cried chokingly, her voice muffled against the rough material of his tailored jacket. 'Oh, Kyle! You never made it quite clear what you had in mind for me, but here I am, and God knows I have no pride left. Take me if you still want me. I love you so much that I'll do anything you want, and be anything you want, and for just as long as you want.'

'That's quite a confession you've just made, Tricia,' he said at length, offering her his handkerchief with which to wipe away her tears.

'I know,' she sniffed into the expensive white linen.

'Does that mean that you will agree to become my mistress?'

Everything seemed to still within her, and then, unable to raise her eyes any higher than the knot in his striped tie, she asked softly, 'Is—is that what you really want?'

'It could be.'

She moaned shakily, turning away from him to stare down into the electric fire while she tried to assuage the pain of her disappointment.

'It could also be that I want you to marry me,' she heard him say abruptly after a brief, tense silence, and she swung round to face him, her dark eyes wide and questioning in her pale face.

'Kyle?'

The expression in his eyes remained unfathomable, but his mouth twisted into a derisively mocking smile. 'Does that appeal to you more?'

Her heart was beating so fast that it almost choked her, and there was a note of anguish in her voice as she begged, 'Don't torment me like this, Kyle. Tell me what you want of me, but don't torment me.'

He was beside her in an instant, his eyes glittering with suppressed fury, and his mouth drawn into a hard, thin line as he gripped her wrists with ungentle fingers and dragged her roughly against him. 'Do you think I wasn't tormented at the thought of you marrying someone else while everything in me cried out for you?' he demanded harshly.

'Oh, Kyle, I——'

'Do you think I enjoyed visualising another man making love to you while my arms ached to hold you?'

His eyes blazed down into hers the one minute, and the next she was caught up in his arms, her softness crushed against him as his angry mouth swooped down to take possession of hers. His kiss was a punishment she endured without complaint, but, when his anger drained from him, his mouth moved over hers hungrily, taking the sweetness they offered, and she locked her arms about his neck, clinging to him rapturously as she returned his kisses with a matching hunger.

'Good God!' he groaned at last, burying his face against her throat and inhaling the delicate perfume he always associated with her. 'There were times during these past weeks when I felt murderous enough to get into my car and drive out to

Knysna for the sole purpose of throttling the life out of Frank Carlson.'

'Forgive me, Kyle,' she whispered softly, brushing her hand over his hair until her fingers rested in the nape of his strong neck.

'Forgive you?' he asked hoarsely as he raised his head, and his tortured expression tore at her heart. 'Tricia, my darling, let's not talk of forgiving. There's so much you have to forgive *me* for that I find it utterly incredible that you can still love me the way you do.'

'I think we won't talk of forgiving again,' she acknowledged gently, noticing for the first time the lines of tiredness etched about his eyes and mouth as her fingers eagerly and lovingly traced the contours of his lean, sometimes harsh face. 'Let's just be thankful for what we have now, and allow the past to bury itself.'

'I wish I could tell you what I feel for you, but there are no words to describe my feelings adequately,' he murmured, drawing her down on to the sofa and into his arms. After another lengthy, satisfying kiss he added, 'To say that I love you sounds so insipid in comparison to what I really feel, but I suppose it will have to do.'

'It will do very nicely, coming from you,' she smiled happily, burying her flushed face against his shoulder.

His fingers moved caressingly along her throat to where a little pulse beat strongly at his touch and, unable to resist the subtle persuasion, she raised her lips to his with an eagerness that ignited his passion.

CHAPTER TEN

THERE was so much still to discuss, but for a long time neither Kyle nor Tricia had the wish to do anything other than to savour each other's lips and arms with a hunger that could not be assuaged and, when desire inevitably throbbed between them, it was Kyle who drew a little away from her.

'You didn't have plans to return to Knysna soon, did you?'

'I hadn't really planned anything, but I brought an overnight bag,' she replied, her cheeks flushed and her dark eyes misty from his lovemaking. 'I saw a nice little hotel not far from here, and——'

'You're staying here in this house, and nowhere else,' Kyle interrupted sternly, his arms tightening about her.

'But, darling, I can't——'

'We're going to be married tomorrow, so what difference would it make?'

'Tomorrow?' she gasped in astonishment and secret delight, her hands against his chest as she leaned back in his arms to search his face and, when she saw the stubbornness in the set of his unrelenting jaw, she asked teasingly, 'Wouldn't that be rushing things a bit?'

His fingers traced the gentle curve of her flushed cheek down to her chin, then they moved exploringly along her slender throat up to her shell-like ear, and the effect was devastating. 'You could say that I've waited six years for this moment, and now I'm not waiting a day longer than I absolutely have to. We're going to be married tomorrow, and no arguments.'

Trying to ignore the sensations created by the sensuality of his touch, she asked, 'What about the board meeting you have to attend tomorrow?'

'The meeting should be over by eleven at the latest. I'll make arrangements for us to be married at two in the afternoon, and after that I'm all yours.'

All yours. The thought sent a shiver of delight through her that made her heart beat faster, and from the devilish expression on Kyle's face she guessed that he was fully aware of what he was doing to her.

'There's my flat,' she argued feebly. 'And I only brought along enough clothing to last the weekend.'

'You can buy whatever clothes you need tomorrow, and when we return home from our honeymoon you can make arrangements about vacating your flat and having your personal things transported to Cape Town.'

'Are we going on a honeymoon?' she asked in breathless disbelief.

'We certainly are,' he said, his lips brushing against hers tantalisingly. 'We're going to a little place along the south coast of Natal where it's usually warm this time of the year, but not too warm for you to sleep in my arms.'

'When did you decide that?' she asked, a deep flush surging from her throat up into her cheeks.

'Just a few minutes ago.'

'Oh, Kyle!' she sighed ecstatically, and then her lips parted for his kiss.

She could not quite believe what was happening to her, but she was suddenly quite content to leave her future in Kyle's strong, capable hands; hands that were caressing her now with an urgency that sent wild and exciting emotions cascading through her.

His fingers did not fumble as he undid the buttons of her jacket and slipped it off her shoulders. His jacket and tie followed hers on to the carpeted floor, and then his heart was thudding into hers through the thinness of his shirt as he pressed her down on to the sofa with his weight. His mouth never left hers throughout this entire procedure, making coherent thought virtually impossible, but when she felt his warm, caressing hands against her skin beneath her sweater, she moved protestingly beneath him.

'Kyle ...' she gasped eventually when his mouth left hers to explore the sensitive areas below her ear. 'About that hotel.'

'Do you really want to go there?'

'Not particularly, but——'

'Then stay.'

His fingers strayed persuasively along the hollow of her back, and as her body arched towards his of its own volition, she asked a little frantically, 'Do you think that's wise? My staying here, I mean?'

'Perhaps not wise,' he laughed softly, teasing the corner of her quivering mouth with his lips, 'but I can promise you an infinitely more satisfying night than the one you would spend in that nice, respectable little hotel you've mentioned.'

'That's what I'm afraid of,' she admitted in a voice husky with emotion.

'You've got nothing to lose, and so much to gain.'

'Kyle . . .'

His mouth shifted purposefully over hers, stifling her protests effectively, and the deliberate sensuality of his kiss was a drain on her resistance, tempting her to surrender herself to the ecstasy she had known once before.

'Say "yes", my love,' he urged finally against her lips, his voice rough with desire.

'I shouldn't,' she persisted, clinging to his shoulders as well as her crumbling sanity.

'But you're going to,' he added persuasively just as the catch of her bra gave way beneath his fingers, then he laughed softly and brought his hands round to cup the firm swell of her breasts.

Those probing, caressing fingers sent a flood of desire raging through her that made her hands tighten on his shoulders where the muscles rippled beneath her touch. 'You're making it awfully hard for me to refuse.'

His lips teased hers lightly, almost tantalisingly. 'Then you're going to say "Yes"?'

'Kyle . . .' she murmured helplessly, intoxicated by the heat of his body against her own, and those hard, muscular thighs pressing into hers, but then, as his lips travelled with a demanding urgency along the sensitive cord of her throat, she knew that she did not want it this way. 'Kyle,' she pleaded softly and urgently, 'don't make me, darling.'

For a moment he did not respond, then his hands stilled along their path of destruction, and he raised his head to look down at her, his tawny eyes darkened with desire, but also a little incredulous. 'Tricia?'

'Let's do things in their proper order,' she pleaded gently, framing his face with her hands. 'Please, Kyle?'

She saw the desire ebb slowly from his glance to make room for understanding, and then he was looking at her with a warmth and tenderness in his eyes that held her spellbound with incredulous wonder.

'As you wish, my love,' he said at last, dropping a light kiss on the tip of her small nose before he got to his feet and moved towards the electric fire to stand with his back to her, and she knew by the set of his shoulders that he was finding it equally difficult to regain his composure. 'There are a choice of rooms at your disposal, and you needn't be afraid to use any of them,' he said at last, adding with a hint of amusement in his voice, 'I don't think it will kill me to exercise a little control until you're legally mine.'

After restoring a certain amount of order to her appearance, Tricia stood up and touched his arm lightly as she whispered, 'Thank you.'

He turned then and, taking her hands in his, he raised them to his lips, and she smiled tremulously, making no effort to hide her love for him as she raised her eyes to his. His fingers tightened momentarily about hers, then he set her firmly aside to refill their glasses.

Tiredness began to overwhelm her and, when she had emptied her glass of wine, she lowered her head on to the backrest of the chair and closed her eyes, but she opened them again hastily a few seconds later when something heavy dropped into her lap. It was her handbag, and Kyle was bending over her, a tender smile softening the often sensorious curve of his mouth.

'Give me the keys to your car. I want to collect your overnight bag and get Samuel to tow your car out of the ditch before I show you up to your room,' he instructed her.

'I'm sorry,' she murmured tiredly, finding her keys and handing them over. 'I guess I've been affected by the long drive from Knysna, and, added to that, I've had too much wine.'

'And too much of my intoxicating presence.'

'And too much of your intoxicating presence,' she repeated with a lazy, humorous laugh as she looked up into his eyes and saw the devilment lurking there.

Their laughter died the next instant, and their eyes clung, speaking a language of their own and, tired as she was, her arms opened wide to receive Kyle. They kissed deeply, and hungrily, their arms straining each other close, and then, with gentle reluctance, Kyle set her free.

'Don't go away,' he whispered unnecessarily, the banked down fires in his eyes making them glitter strangely, and the next moment she was alone.

Five days later Tricia and Kyle were soaking up the winter sun on a secluded section of the beach along the southern coast of Natal, and there was a plain gold band on the finger of her left hand to make the incredible dream a reality.

Thinking back to the night she had arrived at Kyle's home still made her head spin at the speed with which everything had happened. Kyle had kept his word, and she had slept alone in one of the guest rooms in the east wing that night. They had breakfasted together the following morning, uncaring about the curious and questioning glances of the servants, and then they had parted company, Kyle to attend the board meeting while Tricia went out to buy an extensive wardrobe for their two week honeymoon. Samuel, the manservant who had admitted her on her arrival, had managed to manoeuvre her car out of the ditch at the gate, and it had stood waiting for her in the driveway when she left the house.

The rain had ceased during the night, and the sky had cleared miraculously to match Tricia's happy mood while she flitted from one shop to the other, very nearly depleting her bank balance in the process since she had stubbornly refused to accept the cheque Kyle had offered her. On her return to the house she had made a hasty telephone call to Charles and Milly to set their minds at rest and to tell them of her decision to marry Kyle, but after that she hardly had time to think of anything other than preparing herself for the most important moment of her life.

They had been married that afternoon at two o'clock, and not in the impersonal atmosphere of the magistrate's office as she had expected, but in a small church not far from Kyle's home with an elderly clergyman officiating, and two of Kyle's closest friends as witnesses. Afterwards they had flown to Durban where a car had been placed at Kyle's disposal for the journey further south, and now, after four days of sublime happiness, she still found it difficult to believe that she had not dreamt it all.

She rolled over on to her side, raising herself up on to her elbow to study the tanned, muscular body of the man lying beside her on the warm sand and, as always, her heart quickened at the sight of him. He looked almost boyish with his silvery hair lying across his broad forehead, and with his chiselled features free of the tautness which she had seen there so often in the past. Her gaze travelled along the tanned column of his strong neck down to where the short fair hair curled softly on his broad chest and, in a mischievous mood, she trickled a handful of sand on to his flat stomach. His silvery lashes flew upwards, and the next instant their positions were reversed. She found herself lying flat on her back with Kyle leaning over her, his wide shoulders spread out above her to blot out the sun, and his arms imprisoning her while he looked down at her with a devilish sparkle in his tawny eyes.

'Not here, Kyle,' she protested anxiously, guessing his intentions at once, but his lips descended, and she was kissed with a thoroughness that left her breathless, and trembling.

'You spoiled my dream,' he accused her with mock severity.

'Did I?'

'I dreamt we were married.'

'Idiot!' she laughed, running her hands lightly over his chest and loving the springiness of the hair beneath her fingers, but when she felt his heartbeat quicken beneath her hands, she pushed him away and sat up with her back to him.

Her mood changed abruptly as she stared at the foamy waves breaking on the smooth, sandy beach. The flick of Kyle's lighter told her that he had lit a cigarette, and the aroma of his particular brand of tobacco filled her nostrils while he sat up beside her and smoked in silence. They had stoically avoided any serious discussions during the past four days since their marriage, and it was almost as if they had come to the mutual decision not to spoil their first few days of togetherness by discussing the un-happiness of the past, but Tricia could no longer brush aside the questions which clamoured to be answered.

'Kyle,' she began, drawing patterns idly in the sand with her finger, 'I don't particularly want to discuss Maxine, but when did you begin to suspect that she was not what you'd believed her to be?'

If Kyle was surprised at the unexpectedness of her query, he gave no indication of it as he pushed the remainder of his cigarette into the sand and drew her back against him so that his lips almost brushed against her ear as he spoke.

'I think it must have been when my father's will was read,' he explained. 'My father had appointed me the administrator of her inheritance until she was twenty-five, and the will stipulated that if there should be any suspicion of misconduct attached to Maxine's behaviour she would have to forfeit her inheritance. That had sounded odd to me at the time, but I understand it now.'

Tricia also realised now why Maxine had con-sidered it so imperative that she should remain silent about the part Maxine had played in her stepfather's death, and she asked tentatively, '*Has* she forfeited her inheritance entirely?'

'I haven't decided.'

His voice was cold and clipped, but the hand

caressing her smoothly tanned shoulder gave her the necessary courage to say, 'She's your sister, Kyle.'

'My *step*sister, you mean.'

'Let's not split hairs. I know you still care for her very much.'

His hand tightened on the fragile bones of her shoulder as he demanded harshly, 'After what she did to my father, and not to mention to us?'

For a moment she did not speak while she pondered the situation, then she turned and, using his raised knee as a prop for her back, she raised her hand confidently and smoothed away the deep furrows between his eyes with gentle fingers.

'Forgive her, darling,' she pleaded softly.

'Why should I?' he demanded, growing taut beneath her touch as she lightly trailed her fingers down to his square, resolute jaw.

'Because I'm so happy at this moment that I could forgive her anything, and I would like to think you feel the same way too.'

His tight-lipped expression did not alter for a moment as he stared down into the warmth of her unfaltering dark gaze, then he caught her trailing hand in his own and buried his lips against her soft palm.

'Perhaps I'll make arrangements for her to receive a yearly allowance.'

'That's much better,' she smiled, delicious little tremors rushing through her as he kissed each of her fingers in turn and, when he buried his lips against her palm once more, she curled her fingers slightly to caress his cheek. 'Why were you so suspicious of me when we first met? Was it only because of the experience your father had had with women after your stepmother's death?'

'It was partly that, I suppose,' he admitted, frowning heavily. 'I told myself you were a girl from nowhere, a nobody, and money had to be the reason why you latched on to my father, but now I think it must have been a kind of built-in defence mechanism. I was attracted to you, and I didn't particularly enjoy the idea because I valued my freedom too much at the time.' The faintly derisive smile died on his lips as he slid a caressing hand along her arm and across her smooth shoulder to the nape of her neck. 'I tried very hard to forget you during the past six years, but I never quite succeeded.'

'There must have been other women in your life,' she suggested, half in earnest, half in jest.

'There were several.'

His abrupt, but truthful reply temporarily robbed her of speech. Kyle was an attractive man, and she had not really imagined that he had lived the life of a celibate during the past six years, but hearing him admit it was something else. She was aware that he was observing her with a faintly mocking expression in his eyes while he waited for her to say something, and suddenly she knew that it would be childish of her to allow this knowledge to hurt her in any way.

'Should I be jealous?' she asked lightly, and then she was being clasped roughly against his chest.

'No,' he stated emphatically against her quivering mouth. 'They meant nothing to me at all, and now I have no need of anyone else but you—for ever.'

With total disregard for anyone who might choose to walk along that stretch of beach, he kissed her lingeringly, and with a tenderness that made the happiness flow through her veins like intoxicating wine.

She was flushed and trembling when she eventually drew away from him and asked, 'Did you know I was working for Charles Barrett when you bought the mill?'

'Why do you think I made my offer so tempting that Charles would have been a fool to refuse it, and why do you think I took the trouble to organise the take-over personally when I could have sent someone else to do all the dirty work, so to speak?' he demanded with a touch of the old arrogance and, looking down into her questioning eyes, he added, 'I had to see you again somehow without making it too obvious how I felt about you.'

'As I recall, you didn't appear to be very pleased to see me,' she accused humorously, a thrill of pleasure racing through her as his fingers trailed a sensuous path from the hollow of her throat down to where her bikini exposed the cleavage between her breasts.

'If I'd given way to my feelings I would have dragged you out behind that desk, and into my arms. That's why I didn't dare touch you when you held out your hand,' he explained roughly. 'I wonder if you'll ever realise that I went through a private hell of my own, just as you did. I loved you, and I hated myself for it because of what I thought you'd done. Seeing you again after all those years I began to sense that you knew more than you were willing to tell. I knew somehow that it was important for me to discover the reason for your often cynical observations, so I drove you hard, and in every possible way, hoping you would crack. It didn't take me long to discover that Maxine had something to do with it, but I couldn't figure it out until that day she came to the office.' He seemed to pale at the memory. 'It was as if the shades had been lifted from my eyes, and what I saw made me feel *sick*.'

'Kyle ...' she began tentatively, remembering her own misery that day, but he continued to speak as if she had not interrupted, and his tortured expression seared her heart like the thrust of a sword.

'I knew the truth then, but the truth merely drove you further away from me,' he said, and his eyes took on a haunted expression as he added hoarsely, 'I don't think I've ever been so scared in all my life.'

She framed his face gently with her hands, and her heart was in her eyes when she said softly, 'I love you, Kyle.'

'Oh, God!' he groaned, self-derision twisting his handsome features. 'I don't deserve your love, Tricia, I——'

She silenced him hastily with a kiss and, with her arms locked about his neck, she continued to kiss him until she felt his lips move warmly and responsively against her own. The kiss lengthened, became passionate and demanding, and somehow she found herself lying on the sand with the hard length of Kyle's body against her own.

'Do you know what you're doing to me, woman?' he demanded eventually as he dragged his lips from hers to bury them against the softness of her throat where he could feel that tell-tale pulse throbbing frantically at his touch.

'I've a pretty good idea,' she replied tremulously, moving her hands caressingly over his broad back and loving the feel of those muscles rippling beneath his smooth, warm skin.

'Let's go back to the hotel,' he suggested at length, desire flaring in his eyes and, nodding silently, she disengaged herself from his arms to gather up their towels and beach robes.

That night, when they went to bed, Kyle seemed to be in a curiously detached mood and, instead of taking her into his arms as he had done every night since their marriage, he folded his hands behind his head and lay frowning up at the white ceiling of their hotel suite. Tricia observed him from beneath her lowered lashes, sensing his disturbed thoughts, and not quite sure what to do about it.

'Tricia ...' he began at last and, for some inexplicable reason, she stiffened beside him as she waited for him to speak. 'That money my father left you.'

'I don't want to talk about it,' she interrupted hastily before he could say anything further on the subject which was still distasteful to her and, as she sat up in bed, all the old feelings returned; the hurt, the longing and despair, and, placing her hands childishly over her ears, she begged, 'Please, let's not talk about it.'

'I'm going to talk about it, and you're going to listen to me,' Kyle insisted with a harshness that made her flinch as he drew her down into his arms, and steely fingers removed her hands from her ears. 'Look at me,' he ordered sharply when she closed her eyes and turned her head away and, obeying reluctantly, she met that compelling gaze which could caress and punish at will. 'That twenty thousand was invested for you, and it's been chalking up a sizeable interest over the years.'

'I'm not interested,' she protested, struggling beneath him to gain her freedom, but those muscular arms merely tightened about her, and those tawny eyes issued a warning which instantly subdued her.

'My father meant you to have that money. It's yours, Tricia, and it would make me happy if you would accept it.'

She *could* not accept it, not even to please him, she realised with a touch of the old bitterness, but then she thought of that gloomy, disused west wing of his family home in Cape Town. It was in a sad state of disrepair as a result of being shut up since his stepmother's death, and those rooms were simply begging to be lived in once more.

'I'll accept that money on one condition,' she began tentatively, trying to suppress the excitement within her at what she hoped to do.

'What condition?' he frowned suspiciously.

'That you allow me to do with the money as I wish.'

'I smell a rat,' he laughed unexpectedly, 'but explain yourself.'

Her heart was beating in her throat now as she said: 'I'd like to donate some of that money to the orphanage where I lived as a child, and with the rest I'd like to open up the west wing of your home.'

'*Our* home,' he corrected her.

'Our home,' she acknowledged readily. 'I thought one of those rooms could be done up as a nursery, because I'm hoping we'll need one at some future date.' She traced a bold finger along the side of his rigid jaw, and smiled persuasively. 'Are we in agreement?'

'I suppose I shall have to agree if that's the only way I can get you to accept your inheritance,' he sighed resignedly.

He kissed her lightly on the lips, and then again with increasing passion until she clung to him in breathless surrender.

'There will be babies,' he murmured against her lips with a certain urgency.

'I'm hoping so,' she whispered shakily, her body responding deliriously to the intimacy of his caresses.

'Little girls with brown eyes and dark, curly hair like their mother's.'

'And little boys with their father's fair hair and peculiar cat-like eyes,' she whispered teasingly.

'I have so much to make up to you for.'

'Hush,' she silenced him with her fingers against his warm, seeking lips, then she brushed his silvery hair away from his tanned forehead with a tenderness that was reflected in her eyes. 'It's all in the past now, remember? We agreed on that, and the past has no place in the future.'

'You're right,' he muttered throatily, switching off the light. 'No place at all.'

His lips found hers in the darkness while his hands moulded her softness against him and, with an ecstatic little sigh, she surrendered herself to the demands he was making on her. There would be no more talk after this, she knew, but neither of them would ever forget how close they had come to throwing away their happiness.

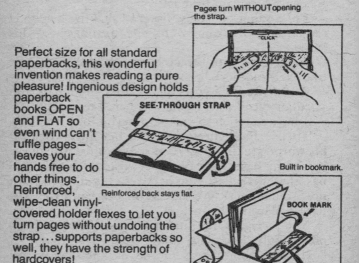